Rain pounded on the roof; the wind rattled whatever was loose to rattle. Gradually the girl in the coffin began to breathe. Slowly, shedding more flakes of styrofoam, she sat up and opened her eyes. The pupils were an intense blue.

"I . . . guess I've . . . passed away," she said in a faint voice. "Otherwise I wouldn't be here."

Jake took hold of her right hand. "I'm Jake Pace," he said, "and this is my wife, Hildy. We'll help you as much as we can."

Hildy smiled at her. "What do you want Odd Jobs, Inc. to do for you, Miss Kirkyard?"

"Well, first off," replied Sylvie, "I want you to find out who murdered me."

BRAINZ, INC.

Ron Goulart

DAW BOOKS, INC.

DONALD A. WOLLHEIM, PUBLISHER

1633 Broadway, New York, NY 10019

First Printing, May 1985

1 2 3 4 5 6 7 8 9

PRINTED IN U.S.A.

 **1**

When the warning alarm went off, Jake Pace was in the kitchen baking cookies and his wife was in their large living room playing Mozart on the banjo.

It was a gloomy, storm-wracked afternoon in the autumn of 2004, with dusk already drifting across their secured estate in the Redding Ridge Sector of Connecticut. An exuberant wind was whipping at the maples and evergreens, tossing hard rain at the Paces' sprawling glaz and redwood home. Thunder rumbled just beyond the surrounding woodlands and lightning crackled.

At every flash the kitchen computer said, "Eek!"

"Hush," advised Jake. He was a long lean

man in his middle thirties, tanned and weather-worn.

"Electromagnetic pulse is going to fry my brains," predicted the voxbox just below the small display screen. "I'll go all gaga and forget completely the twenty thousand exciting and delicious recipes stored within my—"

"Silence." Jake scowled at the terminal while he dumped a second measuring cup of carob chips into his mixing bowl.

"Not that my vast internal knowledge is of much avail. You persist in ignoring my advice even in—"

"All great chefs extemporize."

"You simply can't substitute maple syrup granules for sugar in the recipe for Dockwalloper Carob Chip Cookies and expect . . . Eek!" The recipe on the screen went fuzzy for an instant.

"You two squabbling again?" called Hildy from the next room.

"Just a doctrinal debate," replied Jake.

Hildy resumed her electric banjo rendition of "Eine Kleine Nachtmusik."

"I wonder," mused the sinkside kitchen computer, "how many other heads of nation-ally famous private detective agencies are whip-ping up batches of cookies this aft—"

"Gloomy weather always puts me in the mood for homemade cookies." Bending slightly, Jake shook a little nutmeg into his cookie dough.

"And this sort of day also puts me in an edgy mood, so don't—"

Bbbrrrrinnnnggggg!

"Trouble!" said Hildy.

Jake reached toward the nearby refrig unit, snatched free the spare stungun magnetically stuck to the side of it.

Spinning, he ran from the kitchen and into the living room.

Hildy had already grabbed out the stungun she kept in the lid of her banjo case. Pistol in hand, she was crouched near the wide viewindow that looked out on their acre of rain-battered front lawn.

Bbbbrrrinnnnggggg!

Jake paused in the middle of this possible emergency, to take an admiring look at his wife. She was tall, slender and auburn-haired. One of the most attractive women he'd ever encountered. "Spot anything out there?"

"Unauthorized skycar is coming in over the trees," Hildy replied. "Do we have anyone who's especially eager to do us in at the moment?"

"I could probably draw up a fairly substantial list of folks who're disgruntled with Odd Jobs, Inc." He knelt to the left of her. "But most of 'em aren't dippy enough to come barreling right in here like this."

The intruding skycar was a good nine years old, battered and once black. It was now circling the lawn, low to the ground, in a very offkilter way.

"Think it might be a drone?" suggested Jake. "Loaded with explosives and set to—"

"Nope, it's merely that crazed Irishman." She stood, brushed at her short neosilk skirt.

"You mean that lush John J. Pilgrim?"

Hildy nodded. "Who else flies a skycar that way, forgets to call ahead and let us know he's . . . Oops!"

The flying car had nearly collided with the plazdome over their docking port. Its landing gear grated and slurped across the rain-slick surface and the car lurched, swooped, headed for the ground.

Its battered nose plowed up about ten feet of nugrass and mud before the skycar came to a thumping, rattling stop just short of plunging over into the outdoor pool.

"Yep, it's Pilgrim." Jake slid the stungun into his pocket. "I'll go out and give him the heaveho."

"Find out what he wants, and you better leave the gun here," advised his wife. "I don't want you stunning John J. or—"

"He's perpetually stunned." Sighing, Jake tossed the gun onto a floating coffee table. "How he can continue to get work as an attorney is beyond—"

"He's a very dedicated man."

"Dedicated to booze." Jake's shoulders hunched as he headed for the downramp that led to the ground-level doorway.

"He did help out when you got arrested during that Big Band Murder Case business," reminded Hildy as she followed her lanky husband.

The rain came slapping at Jake when he opened the lower door. "What's the reason for this intrusion, Pilgrim?" he shouted at the nosed-over skycar.

Pilgrim was emerging, backwards, out of the vehicle. A small red-haired man in a rumpled two-piece bizsuit, he was singing to himself as he came toppling out into the mud.

"Oh, I ain't the cosmonaut and I ain't the cosmonaut's son . . . Geeze, did I land on my pinot noir?" Pilgrim struggled to his knees, slapped at his hip pocket and then extracted a plazflask of red wine.

"Unk," commented Jake, watching the red-headed lawyer from their doorway. "He's still guzzling Chateau Discount brand wine."

"And I ain't the cosmonaut's son, but I can explore your black hole till the cosmonaut comes." On his feet finally, swaying, buffeted by the heavy rain, Pilgrim reached into his tipped over skycar and fetched out a black umbrella. "Oh, I ain't the immunologist, and . . . Hey, needlenose, instead of standing over there gawking, give me a hand, okay?" He was pointing the rusted ferrule of his umbrella at Jake.

"Go help him, Jake," urged Hildy. "And, please, don't poke or pummel him."

Jake's only reply was a martyred snort. Inhaling, he sprinted for the wobbly attorney. The wind and the rain attacked him, pushing him back. "C'mon, I'll guide you into the house," he offered, teeth close to gritting. "Then you can explain why it is you've come barging into our—"

"Get your clammy mitts off me, Pace." In jerking free, the small lawyer bonked against the side of his landcar, stumbled, went down on his knees in the rain. "It's not my dapper, compact person I wish help with." He shoved the umbrella open, raised it over his rainsmeared red head. The wind sucked the umbrella free of his grasp, took it dancing away into the thickening twilight. "Gar, you're jinxed, Pace. I've had that darn parasol for near to nine years and never had a single mishap. Then I come paying a—reluctant, I can assure you, old pal—business visit on you and my—"

"What exactly is the reason for your dropping in?"

Pilgrim scowled, pointing in at the rearseat of his downed skycar. There was a large coffin-like neowood crate lying on it at an awkward angle. "I have brought you this, acting on the instructions of my late client," he explained, spitting into his palms and rubbing them together. "Now help me tote the darn thing into your seedy ménage."

The thunder seemed to be rolling nearer; the ground shook.

"What's in it?" Jake reached in, got a grip on the big crate.

"A body," replied Pilgrim. "More or less."

Jake worked at prying the lid off the crate with a crowbar.

The lid made a mournful, keening noise.

Outside fresh lightning flashed, turning everything pale crackling blue.

"Care for a little nip, Hildy?" The red-haired lawyer held his flask toward her while they stood around the crate in the center of the living room. "Chateau Discount pinot noir fortified with cranberry juice cocktail and—"

"No, thanks, John J."

As the lid came all the way free, Hildy peered down into the shadowy interior of the coffinlike box.

"Planning to have seafood for dinner this evening, perhaps? White wine'll go better with that. Somewhere about my damp person I have a flagon of Chateau Discount chablis with added prune juice from concentrate that—"

"That's Sylvie Kirkyard," realized Hildy.

Jake brushed the rest of the styrofoam potato chips off what appeared to be the body of a blonde young woman in her late twenties. "A reasonable facsimile, actually," he said.

Pilgrim took a swig from his red wine flask. " 'Twas the dear lass' final wish that I deliver this thing to you," he told them, wiping his lips on his soggy coat sleeve. "A real pain in the toke it's been, too, sneaking around and doing all sorts of sly and danger—"

"Why?" inquired Jake.

"Because she didn't want anyone to know. Not a single one of her grasping, conniving relations nor, yet again, any of her many mercenary, albeit socially prominent, suitors."

"I meant," said Jake, stepping back from the box, "why did the heiress to one of the world's largest, vastest electronics fortunes want us to have this android sim of her?"

Pilgrim tapped the side of his head. Since he used the hand holding the wine bottle, some of the pinot noir sloshed on him and dribbled down onto the carpeting. "You've heard of Brainz Inc. I assume?"

"It's a branch of Kirktronics," said Hildy as she looked in again at the lifelike android that seemed to be sleeping on a bed of styrofoam chips. "Her younger brother is the president of

Brainz, Inc., her elder brother is the chairman of the board and Sylvie was also on the board."

Jake began to circle, slowly, the crate. "Brainz, Inc.'s technicians worked out a way to transfer the complete and entire contents of a human brain to a tiny silicon chip called a mindspot," he said as he prowled. "They can then plant that chip in the skull of a fairly convincing andy simulacrum of your body." He snapped his fingers. "Immortality. Of sorts."

Pilgrim was prodding himself beneath the left arm in search of yet another of his spare flasks. "Imagine wanting to drag on your darn life forever," he said, shaking his head and sending out drops of rain. "At any rate, the big snag thus far has been the blooming cost of the Brainz, Inc. process. Runs in the neighborhood of fifty million for the whole package. Thus most of their customers so far have been wealthy business moguls, wealthy politicians and wealthy show-biz luminaries who yearn to continue beyond their spans." Locating the bottle he was seeking, Pilgrim tugged it out into the open. "Ah, Chateau Discount sparkling burgundy laced with root beer. A feast for the—"

"Sylvie Kirkyard," said Jake, ceasing his pacing, "was about twenty-seven when she died last week. That's sort of young to have been thinking about her—"

"She apparently'd been having intimations of mortality," said Pilgrim.

"She was a very pretty young woman," remarked Hildy. "Shame she died in a stupid accident like that, so young. The aircirc system in her underground villa in the Greater Los Angeles area went on the fritz and she suffocated before—"

"Why us?" Jake asked of the tipsy lawyer. "Why'd she want this replica delivered to us?"

"That you'll have to learn from the gadget herself. I am simply carrying out instructions."

"When was this sim made?" Hildy asked.

"Six months ago, on the sly. She made use of the services of a couple of trusted long-time employees." The wobbly Pilgrim unscrewed the cap of his flask. "You both know, don't you, how the Brainz, Inc. service works? You go in for the original mindspot transfer, which takes nearly a day. Then once a month thereafter you have to drop in at any one of twenty-six posh locations around this giddy globe for what they call an update session. That adds all your most recent thoughts and memories to the mindspot. Otherwise, if you, say, didn't kick off until ten years after having the original chip made, there'd be a large mental gap."

"The point of this discourse is?" asked the impatient Jake.

"How can such a fair flower as yourself put up with this dim bulb, Hildy?"

"He bakes admirable cookies."

"I bet he does." After a long appreciative guzzle from his newfound sparkling burgundy, the sozzled attorney continued. "Sylvie Kirkyard had a mindspot copy of her brain made, again without the knowledge of her kith and kin, six months ago. Each month she snuck back for an update. Her death last week caught her several days shy of her next session, meaning there's a three-week gap twixt what the late Sylvie Kirkyard knew and what this fetching gadget has in her coco."

"Is that important?" asked Hildy.

"Might be, might be." He returned his attention to his wine.

Jake leaned over the crate. "Let's get her activated."

"There's an instruction booklet buried in that stuff someplace," said Pilgrim.

"Won't need it." Jake reached beneath the front of the young woman's tunic, pressed a small indentation between her breasts. Withdrawing his hand, he stood back and away.

The rain pounded on the roof, the wind rattled whatever was loose to rattle.

Gradually the android began to breathe. Slowly, shedding more flakes of styrofoam, she sat up and opened her eyes. The pupils were an intense blue.

"I . . . guess I've . . . passed away," she said in a faint voice as she glanced carefully around. "Otherwise I wouldn't be here."

Jake took hold of her right hand. "I'm Jake Pace," he said, "and this is my wife, Hildy. We'll help you as much as we can."

Hildy smiled at her. "What do you want Odd Jobs, Inc. to do for you, Miss Kirkyard?"

"Well, first off," replied Sylvie, "I want you to find out who murdered me."

 **2**

Hildy handed the pretty android a plyochief. "Here, use this."

"Thank you." Sylvie dabbed at her tear-stained cheeks. "I wasn't nearly this maudlin when I was alive."

"Talking about your own death," said Jake, "is bound to unsettle you a mite."

After blowing her completely believable nose, she said, "I suspect Oscar, bless him, built this sim a bit more sentimental than—"

"Who's Oscar?" asked Jake.

They had settled, after helping the android replica of Sylvie Kirkyard out of the crate, in the below ground family room. Jake slouched in a licorice-hued glaz rocker, Hildy and the android shared a plaz sofa facing him. John J. Pilgrim was sprawled, Roman orgy attendee style, on the bench in front of Jake's upright white piano.

"Oscar McCracklin, who runs the R&D Department for our Brainz, Inc. division," answered Sylvie. "He's one of the two people in the whole darn Kirktronics organization I trust. Oscar built this body for me and installed the mindspot."

Jake asked her, "Who's the other one you trust?"

"That'd be Dr. Rose Sanhamel," said the blond android. "Rose is in charge of our Malibu Sector Brainz, Inc. salon in Greater Los Angeles." Sylvie touched at her temple. "She made the mindspot for me ... for me when I was a person, I mean. Gee, it's tough getting used to the idea I'm dead and gone."

"But you aren't really," said Hildy. "You have all your memories and—"

"Heck, though, all I really am is a sort of transcription." Sylvie hugged herself, shivering. "I hadn't counted on it being so spooky. Sylvie Kirkyard is dead and yet—"

"Legally, Toots," put in the lawyer, "you can still do just about everything you did before. Thanks to your own Kirktronics lobby both the Live Congress and Computer Congress passed a law five years ago. The Robotic Proxy Act. A sim with a Brainz, Inc. chip in its cabeza carries on the business and legal functions of the original person.''

"You could then," said Hildy, watching the android, "simply go back to your family business and do the same jobs you were doing before—''

"No, I can't," she said quickly. "Not yet."

"But legally—''

"She's afraid they'll bump off the andy," explained Pilgrim, producing a flask of wine.

"I didn't come here to get tangled up in a legal, or a metaphysical for that matter, discussion." Sylvie lifted the tunic from her left side and gave herself a sharp whack with her fist. That produced a hollow thump, followed by a hum and then a *ping*. "Being a machine has some advantages, I guess, even though I still am not used to weighing sixteen pounds more than I used to. These little compartments come in handy." From the small drawer that had slid open in her sinflesh side she took a roll of papers. "These should cover your fee."

Hildy unwound the scarlet sewdotwine from the papers the android had dropped in her lap. "Negotiable Bondz, Jake—four hundred thousand dollars' worth."

Sylvie blinked her bright blue eyes. "Is that sufficient?"

"Don't know yet," said Jake. "Let's hear the details of the case first."

"Holy Mulroony," muttered the lawyer. "I have to bust my toke for a whole flapping year to earn that and this gumshow says—"

"But you," reminded Sylvie, nodding at him, "devote a lot of your time to doing volunteer work for Lost Cause, the Hopeless Fund, and other worthwhile things like that. Naturally, being noble, you aren't going to net as much as a crackerjack team of private eyes." She smiled across at Jake. "I first met Mr. Pilgrim at a fund-raiser for some members of the Mexam Agricommandos in the Fresno Sector of GLA. He was going to defend them against a counter-suit brought by Walt Disney Nuclear Power, Inc. Seems the whole mess commenced when the grandmother of one of the farmers was atomized one afternoon when an accident at Goofy Plant #3 caused several square miles of the San Joaquin Valley to—"

"We all agree he's noble," Jake cut in. "Get back to your own problem."

"Well, I just wanted you to know why I trusted Mr. Pilgrim and hired him to deliver me . . . or this facsimile of me to you. I think a man who works for justice rather than reward is—"

"A dimwit," said Jake. "What makes you think you were murdered?"

Smiling, Sylvie touched Hildy's bare arm with her warm, authentic fingers. "I like your husband," she confided. "He's mean, gruff, nasty, sarcastic, snide, cynical. All the things the traditional hard-boiled shamus ought to be."

"Ha," remarked Pilgrim after taking a gulp of wine. "Pace's about as hard-boiled as the lace trim on a pansy's underdrawers." With considerable flailing and grunting, he shifted to a sitting position facing the keyboard.

"Don't play," warned Jake.

The red-haired attorney held up both hands, fingers wide. "They're not dirty," he assured him. "I wiped them on yonder drapes soon as I came in."

"Even so."

Hildy said, "Suppose you tell us how we can help you, Sylvie."

"Start," suggested Jake, "by explaining how the hell you can even be sure you were murdered."

"That's obvious," she said, puzzled. "I'm dead."

"According to the media accounts, your death was an accident," said Jake. "The Law Force of Greater Los Angeles made a very thorough investigation into the—"

"Baloney!" She folded her arms under her convincing breasts. "I read several faxpaper acounts while I was lying low in Oscar's home workshop in the Laguna Sector. It seems obvious to me—"

"They even, at the insistence of one of your bereaved suitors, had the Murder Squad take a look at the circumstances surrounding your—"

"Yes, that was Bert. Poor boy. Well, he's not a boy actually, since thirty-six is getting toward maturity and—"

"Bert who?" Jake showed a trace of impatience.

"Bert Higby. My name's been linked with his so much of late I assumed you—"

"Some kind of cartoonist, isn't he?"

"Actually Bert's a very gifted graphic novelist. He draws the SplatterMan series of—"

"Graphic novelist, my aging fanny." Pilgrim's knobby fingers were hovering over the keys. "Funny books about some crazed ninny who flits around dressed like a ballet dancer while killing or maiming every blessed soul who gets in his—"

"How does your graphic novelist friend tie in?" Jake asked their new client.

"Bert was one of the few men in my life I almost trusted," replied Sylvie. "I didn't tell him about this new body or the mindspot . . . In a way, though, I wish I had. He must be heartbroken."

"Lad's got a forehead about the height of a gnat's pecker," said the tipsy attorney, holding his thumb and forefinger fairly close together.

"His brain, if placed beside a lone and underfed prune pit, would be dwarfed as well as outclassed. He's too dim to be heartbroken."

After frowning at him, Sylvie continued, "I had confided some of my fears and suspicions to poor Bert. That's why he suspected foul play and urged the police to probe."

"They did probe," reminded Jake. "The conclusion was that your death was accidental."

"How's this for a novel notion, Pace? The coppers made a mistake."

"Could be they did," acknowledged Jake. "What I'm trying to get at, though, is some facts that'll help us prove it."

"Well, there's one fact I can give you," said Sylvie. "I was killed because I was getting too close."

"To what?" Hildy asked.

Folding her hands in her lap, she said, "As Mr. Pilgrim may have informed you, my memories, unfortunately, stop twenty-two days before my murder. Nevertheless, I must've found out even more. Something, you know, that scared them enough to have me taken care of."

Jake asked her, "Who exactly are we talking about?"

After running her tongue over her upper lip, Sylvie replied, "Listen, let me backtrack some, okay? That way I can, I hope, convince you I really was murdered."

"Anybody mind if I noodle the 'Cow Cow Boogie' on this second-rate instrument while the lady unburdens herself?" inquired Pilgrim.

"Yes," said Jake. "Don't do it."

"Don't play, John J.," said Hildy.

He scowled at his raised hands before letting them flutter down to his soggy trouser knees. "How about something quieter, like 'Lullabye of Birdland' or 'Misty'?"

"How about I toss you out on your keester into the raging elements?" said Jake.

"Fellas," cautioned Hildy, "let her tell her story."

"I've been waiting, patiently," said Jake, slouching farther in the dark rocker, "for that very thing."

"Likewise," Pilgrim assured them all.

"Go ahead," said Hildy.

And this is the story the blond android told.

Some seven months ago Sylvie had begun to suspect that something was going on wrong within the mammoth Kirktronics empire that she and her two brothers controlled. Specifically the problem had to do with the Brainz, Inc. division.

Sylvie, very cautiously and entirely on her own, began to do some digging. She learned enough to convince her someone was using the Brainz, Inc. setup as part of a sinister conspiracy. When certain key political, business, and entertainment figures came to one of the facilities for brain duping, something else was done. The result, Sylvie was nearly certain, is that many important people are now mind-controlled slaves of someone connected with Kirktronics. Since more important figures are being added each week, Brainz, Inc. may soon be able to control a good deal of the economy of the Earth.

Sylvie was nearly certain that the brilliant technohypnotist, Dr. Vincent Death, was the one who devised the mindcontrol system and introduced it at Brainz, Inc. The only thing that makes her somewhat doubt this is that Dr. Death is such an openly rotten and nasty person that he seems too obvious to suspect. He was hired three years ago by her late Uncle Milford and she believes he is now in cahoots with one of her brothers.

The trouble is, up to the time when the mindspot memory ended, Sylvie hadn't been able to determine whether the rotten apple was her younger brother, Kevin, or the older Ross. She is convinced that some time after her last mindspot update session she did learn more, enough to cause the opposition to murder her and rig it to look like nothing more than an accident.

When she'd concluded her account, Sylvie added, "If you clear the whole mess up, which

I'm absolutely certain you'll be able to do, I'll be happy to pay a bonus of an additional—"

"We'll need an additional hundred thousand right now," Jake told her. "In front."

"Oy," remarked Pilgrim, producing a chord on the piano with his left elbow.

Sylvie smiled. "You'll take my case then?"

Jake nodded. "Sure."

Sylvie opened her side for another $100,000.

3

"These aren't as good as they could be."

"You were distracted."

"That's no excuse." Jake took another cookie from the plate resting on the glaz coffee table.

It was still raining, but the lightning and thunder had ceased and there was only darkness outside.

Hildy said, "You're sure she'll be safe there?"

"Iola, Wisconsin is one of the safest towns in the entire country," he assured her. "A recent survey in the *National Intruder* listed it among—"

"Safe for normal, everyday people. Not necessarily for the android replica of an electronics empire heiress who's already been murdered once."

"Sylvie'll be okay." He took a bite of the cookie.

Hildy uncrossed and recrossed her long, handsome legs. She was sitting across from her husband in a tin sling chair. "Another thing that shakes my confidence a wee bit," she admitted, "is the name of the fellow who's going to shelter her."

"Moneyback Smith's sort of catchy, I think."

"For a used skycar salesman maybe."

"Well, that's what Smith is supposed to be. So the name is apt."

Hildy's pretty nose wrinkled very slightly. "I know you've used him before to hide out witnesses and such, but still—"

"He's one of the most reliable safehouse proprietors around. Relax."

"The guy was arrested last spring."

"For selling hot skycars, not for hiding people out. All part of his cover."

Hildy shrugged, not completely convinced. "Well, I hope John J gets her delivered there safely."

"I put his jalopy on automatic."

"Poor kid, having to travel around in a wooden box like a cadaver."

"That arouses less suspicion. Till we clear things up it's best nobody sees her." He pushed the plate of cookies aside, slid over the small wallvid control box. "I want to look over some of the stuff she told us.".

"You believe her, don't you?"

Jake looked up. "Hey, we don't take a case we don't believe in," he reminded.

"What do we have on Dr. Death in our info files?"

"Not as much as I'd like. I may have to check in with Steranko the Siphoner before too long," said Jake. "I went over our material while my cookies were baking."

"Could he be the mastermind behind the sort of plot Sylvie suspects?"

"Death, Vincent X. Age 42. Lives in the Fort Pasadena Sector of Greater Los Angeles," recited Jake, deciding to have another cookie. "He's been married three times, always to ladies both older and richer than he. Each wife died in an accident, leaving her entire vast estate to him. Matter of fact, each of them died by falling into the Grand Canyon."

"Simultaneously?"

"On three separate occasions."

"Sounds a shade suspicious."

"That's exactly what the Hartford Assurance Society decided about the time the remains of Mrs. Death number three were being gathered up from the bottom of the canyon," said Jake. "But when they voiced their suspicions, Dr.

Death sued them and won. Libel, slander, mental anguish."

"Didn't he also sue some publisher who issued an unauthorized bio a couple years back?"

"Threatened to sue unless all the copies of the tome were recalled," said Jake. "Recalled and then burned in a bonfire in Times Square. Tepid & Sons, on advice of counsel, complied and roasted thirty-seven thousand copies of *Death: Merchant of Death*? Made quite a blaze apparently."

"He sounds like a formidable gent."

Jake nodded. "Just before going to work for Kirktronics he served briefly as the head of the Minnesota Criminal Castration Center. They let him go for being overzealous."

"He got into some mess in Africa, too, didn't he?"

"Nope, he won a medal. That was at the end of a five-year stint as R & D chief in the Crowd Control Lab in White Africa number nineteen," said Jake. "Prior to that Death had been in England, where he invented the sonic birchrod for use in public schools."

"He's been politically active lately, too."

"In the last election he campaigned for Fred Hitler," said her husband.

"The fellow who claimed to be the grandson of Adolph Hitler?"

"The same. Fred Hitler, founder of the Nazi Plus Party." Jake sat back on the sofa.

Hildy sighed faintly. "I'm almost inclined to agree with Sylvie," she said. "Dr. Death sounds too awful and mean to be true."

"Never overlook the obvu."

Hildy asked, "How do you want to break this investigation up?"

Jake nodded at her. "Any ideas?"

"Well, one of us heads for Greater Los Angeles, obviously," she answered. "Pokes into the circumstances surrounding Sylvie's death . . . That's funny. Talking about her death and yet we were with her this afternoon."

"One of the many paradoxes of an advanced tech society. What else?"

"Talk to the two loyal employees who helped her, see if they can fill in any of the blanks in the android's missing memory."

Jake's lean face took on a slightly dubious look. "I'm not sure about a direct approach right off."

"Because one of them may've double-crossed her?"

"Yep, might be."

"Then why didn't the opposition destroy the android sim, too?"

"Something to find out, if either Oscar Mc-Cracklin or Dr. Rose Sanhamel turns out to be less admirable and supportive than Sylvie believes."

Hildy said, "Okay, one of us investigates in GLA and the other starts checking out the people Sylvie suspects of being mind-controlled."

"Right, because whoever's controlling them may be hanging around or at least dropping in on them. And that'll give us a nice clue as to who's who." He flipped a toggle on the control box and the opposite wall blossomed into light. "I want to see that part of our conversation wherein she gave us the names of the possible controlled Brainz, Inc. customers."

". . . and I ain't the avionics consultant's son, but—"

"Fast forward!" Jake pushed another toggle. "I wish to hell that nitwit hadn't started singing and playing the damn piano during the last part of our interview with her."

"The Irish are very musical."

"Here we are."

On the large screen appeared an image of the Sylvie Kirkyard simulacrum. The concealed camera down in the family room had picked her up very well.

". . . including key people in politics, finance, and show business," the blonde was saying. "All of them extremely important and influential."

"Who are they?" Jake had asked.

And Sylvie had named names.

 **4**

Jake's skycar was zooming westward through the clear afternoon. He was passing over Utah when his dash pixphone started beeping.

He flipped the receive switch and Steranko the Siphoner showed up on the saucer-size screen.

"I'm not even going to charge you an extra $500 for this flashy express service, old pal," announced the small, bald information bootlegger. "Not even add $250 to the paltry fee of $1750 we agreed upon last eve when you and your beanpole of a spouse conned me into undertaking a monumental—"

"What have you got on Dr. Death?"

Today Steranko was clad in a two-piece

bizsuit of peanut butter color. He was reclining in a polka-dot neosilk hammock chair in the midst of the homemade computer terminals, databoxes and other electronic tapping equipment that cluttered his headquarters. "That is, it turns out, going to take a mite longer than anticipated," he said, rubbing a beringed hand across his hairless head. "Listen, Jake, are you sure you want me to mess with this chap?"

"I do. What's the—"

"Well, someone has placed some very complex blocks in my way. Complex and expensive blocks that are keeping me, old chum, from accessing the information you seek on his past life and times."

"Who? Government?"

"Naw, did I ever have any trouble getting by a government block?" He shook his head. "This is private, big money private."

"Probably Kirktronics themselves have—"

"Not just them, sweetheart. I sense we're dealing with some powerful—"

"If it's going to be too rough for you to—"

"Did I say, or even imply, that? Don't go acting as dense as your skinny spouse," said the siphoner. "I'll have you a complete dossier on Vince by sundown."

"Sundown in CalSouth or back where you you are?"

"Hanging around so many criminal types has brought out a nasty streak in you, Jacob."

"My clients keep telling me private investigators are supposed to be snide and cynical," said Jake. "What about the GLA police files on the death of Sylvie Kirkyard?"

Shifting in his neosilk chair, Steranko reached beneath it. From among piles of daisy wheels, spools of tape, lopsided rolls of printout paper and sprawls of unclassified debris he plucked an old fashioned manila folder. "Is this what you're investigating—the young lady's demise?"

"That's part of it."

"Gad, we've been bosom buddies for eons, Jacob, and yet you persist in clamming up like a—"

"Bosom buddies wouldn't be my first choice for a phrase to describe our relationship."

"I've saved your miserable life, rescued your dippy wife," reminded Steranko. "Among certain tribes the saving of a life means an eternal bond of—"

"I'm not a member of any of those tribes. What have you dug up on the Kirkyard death?"

The little thirty-year-old siphoner tapped the folder on his knee a few times. "Is somebody trying to pull an insurance scam with this, anything like that?"

"Hell, this early in the case almost anything could be involved. Why?"

"There are some unusual aspects," Steranko said slowly. He fished a glossy photo out of the folder and held it up. "You see this okay on your discount screen?"

"Looks like a picture of a bucket."

"Geeze, what an artistic eye you have. It's an urn."

"So?"

"The urn that held, for a brief while, the ashes of the late Sylvie Kirkyard."

"They cremated her?"

"You know a better way to produce ashes?" He tossed the photo aside and it became part of the clutter surrounding him. "I now hold up a copy of a note left by the young lady among her effects. 'Whenever I may die, please, see that I am cremated and that my ashes are then scattered over the beautiful Pacific Ocean off Oxnard.' "

"Oxnard? How could anyone be sentimental about Oxnard or—"

"She supposedly had fun during grunion runs there in her carefree childhood. Fish nostalgia, though, ain't the point, Baby Dumpling."

"Note's a fake?"

"Bingo, you win a stogie on the first try," said Steranko, chuckling. "The handwriting was produced by a modified Japanese-made letter signing machine. Though it's dated April 5,

2000, the ink is only days old. I'd estimate this dumb thing was concocted after she died."

"And the ashes really have been scattered?"

"From the belly of a glazbottom chopper. At sunset two days after she passed on. Her two brothers and our pal, Doc Death, were the only mourners aboard."

"Somebody wanted to get rid of the body."

Steranko made his eyes go wide. "Wow, Uncle Jake, what a keen insight," he exclaimed, clapping his hands. "Now I know why press and public alike have dubbed you the prince of cerebral sleuths."

"I was more or less talking to myself."

"Keep in mind you need classier dialogue when communicating with me."

"What about the various police investigations into her death?"

Smiling, Steranko opened the folder. "I ran down copies of six reports."

"Six? Why the hell so many—"

"There is the initial Law Force report." He held up a finger. "Next the one that was substituted for it. Then we have the first Murder Squad report and its sub. Lastly a first and second medical report."

"How'd you manage to get hold of the original—"

"Wizards never give away their secrets."

"Can you telefax me copies of everything, to my hotel in GLA?"

"For twenty-five bucks extra, unless you want it sent by the cheaper Info Rate."

"Okay, add twenty-five to your damn voucher."

"I can give you the gist now."

"How much'll that cost extra?"

"Listen, you and I are blood brothers, Jake. This pithy little precis I pass along for *nada*. A freebie. Because of the extreme respect I—"

"I love the preamble. How long before we get to—"

"Patience, patience. Didn't they tell you in gumshoe school that detective work requires much patience?"

Jake said, "Whenever you're ready, Steranko."

"The Law Force investigators found signs, albeit faint, that the aircirc system in her underground suite at the Hidden Acres Estates complex had been tampered with. Expertly done work, yet leaving a few faint telltale signs behind."

"So something, maybe a gas, was introduced into her rooms?"

"Could be." Steranko held up several sheets of thin yellowish paper. "The initial medical report."

"Cause of death?"

"Asphyxia."

"That fits with the accident idea, though. That her aircirc system conked out, the central control malfunctioned and didn't repair it fast enough and she died in her sleep from lack of oxygen."

"The original medic, who is, by the bye, now enjoying an extended vacation in some obscure corner of Central America, was puzzled by a faint orangish tinge to the poor girl's flesh."

Jake sat up in the pilot seat. "Wait now," he said. "That reminds me of something about Dr. Death. When I was scanning our own files on him yesterday I—"

"Is this mayhap what you came across, sunshine?" He waved a tearsheet from a faxmag. "Ran in *Mammon* three years ago. Discusses the doc's halcyon days in Africa controlling the restless blacks."

"Yep, that's it. He perfected a gas called Asthmaline," recalled Jake. "A whiff of the stuff knocked you cold, but too much would . . . smother you, cut off your air supply."

"Be interesting to know if traces of Asthmaline were found in the late Miss Kirkyard's posh suite, eh?"

"It would," agreed Jake, drumming his fingers on the dash. "I want names of all the cops, Law Force and Murder Squad, who were involved in the investigation. Some of the names I already have from the news accounts."

"You figure to find out which ones were bribed and by whom?"

"Seems like the sensible thing to do."

"It do. But, Jacob, mine boy, it's going to require a lot of the aforementioned patience."

"How come?"

"Of the seven GLA officers involved, five are now on extended leaves, scattered to the four corners of the earth," explained the bald siphoner. "Yet another is in the Intensive Care Wing of the Brazilian War Veterans Memorial Hospital in Pacific Palisades. He's in a deep coma."

"And the other guy?"

"No one seems to know where he is anymore," answered Steranko with a grin. "My bet is he was added to the Pacific off Oxnard and is feeding the grunion right this minute."

"Well, I want the names anyway."

"I'll ship 'em with the rest of this stuff," promised the siphoner. "Since we are, as alluded to earlier, staunch comrades, Jake, I feel obliged to offer a bit of sound advice."

"Go ahead," invited Jake.

"Drop this one. You're going up against folks with one hell of a big budget," said Steranko. "Lots of dough and no scruples, that's tough to beat. I'd hate to see you end up in an urn."

Jake grinned and shook his head. "Don't worry. Hildy has instructions to donate my body to science."

5

As the sun was setting over the nation's capital, a glittering silver skycar came whispering down through the dusk to land in the Celeb Sector of the skylot next to the Whoopee Arms. A few of the media people and robot cameras who'd been covering the picketing demonstration in front of the towering glaz and neometal building came trotting over to the lot.

Hildy, decked out in a stunning two-piece white-leather-and-diamonds funsuit, emerged from the cabin of the silvery skycar, long bare legs first. She smiled demurely, fluffed at her long platinum hair and complained, "Ham I to half to peas?"

"She means is she to have no peace," interpreted a black newsman from Int Wallvid.

"What brings you here, Baroness Eed?" asked a CBS robot.

"I font to half zum funn." She smiled at the gathering group as she shut the door of her vehicle with her rump. "But I sink maple I whorive hat tea wronk time, no?"

"Oh, it's just simply another wage action," explained the IW reporter, ogling the lowcut neck of her gem-encrusted tunic. "The Washington Page & Prostitute Federation wants higher wages. And since the United States Secretary of Vice, Mr. Tintin, also resides in this complex they—"

"I don like crossing a piglet line."

"Oh, all the other bordellos, casinos and such in the Whoopee Arms are doing business as usual. It's only Secretary Tintin, up in the penthouse, that the lads are ticked off at."

"I taught Seggretary Tintin wuz haway."

"Sure, Baroness," said the man from NBC Satellite News. "He's over in Arlington dedicating the newest White Slave Discount Whorehouse, but these pansys don't have the sense to—"

"Watch the sexist remarks," warned an ABC robot.

Her sources of information weren't wrong

then. "Fell, I go inzide den." Hildy smiled and pushed her way, gracefully, through the gaggle of newspeople.

"What floor are you going to, Baroness Eed?"

"You muzzle axe such intimate quiztions." She giggled sweetly, letting her long silvery eyelashes flutter.

"Did you whiz over from your native Orlandia just to visit the Whoopee Arms or—"

"I hallzo intent to tog about arms limitations wit your presidunce."

"Do you mean to imply that Orlandia isn't going to allow any further Kilgas missiles to be deployed on its soil and—"

"Sat you half to axe King Rudy." Using her elbows and a knee, Hildy got clear of the media.

The two dozen pickets were marching in a lazy circle in front of the tower building. Their tri-op signs blinked and pulsed, flashing angry slogans into the night.

"You half my zupport," Hildy assured them, elbowing aside a lovely boy who was dressed much as she was.

"Thanks, sweetie pie."

The big lobby of the vice complex was crowded. Customers of the Off Track Betting System were loitering, comparing notes, making use of the robot-manned betting windows. A few freelance teen hookers were trying to hustle. A huge black man who was delivering some of the contestants for the upstairs cockfights was arguing with the elevator captain about why he didn't want to deliver his crate on the service lift. An awed group of tourists was being escorted toward the ground-level snack bar by a Chinese girl guide in a seethru jumpsuit. And five Secret Service men tried, at various strategic positions, to blend. They were here because US Secretary of Vice Lloyd Tintin had the penthouse floor. Even when he was elsewhere, the place was guarded, down here and above.

It made Hildy's job a bit tricky. She had to get to the top public floor, where the gambling casino was, and then sneak up to the—

"Well, well. Hildy Pace. What brings you to DC?"

"You are mistoken. I ham Baroness Eed from—"

"You do look a hell of a lot like her, Mrs. P. Shows what a big budget private op outfit like Odd Jobs, Inc. can do when—"

"I wooden like to call a segurity guard to bop you on the beezer, yet—"

"Go easy, ma'am." The man who'd pushed his way up to her was thin, about fifty-one, wearing an ancient sinwool overcoat. "I have nothing but business in mind." He handed her a dog-eared business card.

WHISPERING WOLFBANGER,
Accredited Informant

"One of DC's best informed sources,"
says High Place Official.

"I gum here to gimble. I do not neat a—"

"The real Baroness Eed happens to be in Cairo, Egypt right now, attending the Fifth Annual Invitational Coke Sniffing and Wine Tasting Festival, dear lady," Whispering Wolfbanger informed her. "These media dolts don't know that, but old WW does. For three hundred dollars I don't tip the Secret Service lads."

"Okay, ride up in the elevator with me," Hildy invited, linking her arm with his. "I'm sure we can make a deal, Mr. Wolfbanger."

The automatic elevator cage they chose was thick with other customers of the Whoopee Arms. As the doors hissed shut, the ceiling vox box requested, "Name your floors, if you please."

"Mama Kandy's Krib," said a Shriner with a fez that blinked on and off.

"Gay Bob's Fag Floor," boomed a beefy sailor.

"Um . . . Fang Gow's . . . um . . . Dope Den," requested a young man who was clinging to the arm of his even younger young woman companion.

"Pain City," stated a thickset woman in a leathette bizsuit.

"What dang floor are the cockfights on, amigo?" asked a broad-chested man in cowboy gear.

"Sixteen, sir."

"That's for me then, doggone it."

Hildy said, "Chez Monaco Gambling Hell."

The elevator said, "Thank you, one and all," and commenced a smooth, silent climb upward.

"I want it in cash," whispered Whispering Wolfbanger. "I imagine an important op such as yourself, Mrs. P. carried a lot more than three hundred in bills on her lovely person. I could ask you for more, you see, but I—"

"No need to explain your business practices." Hildy turned half toward him and raised her diamond-studded purse to chest level. Tilting it toward the anxious informant's face, she opened it.

"Wowie, look at all that cabbage therein . . . in . . . ump . . . caff caff . . . argle . . . you double . . . gah." He slumped against her, eyes shut.

Closing the purse, Hildy asked her fellow passengers, "Is dere a dogturd in the elewaiter?"

"Watch the dirty talk, lady," cautioned the sailor, blushing.

"A dogturd, a dogturd, a madical man. Please."

"She means a doctor, you dim-witted waddie," translated the cowboy, after tipping his high Stetson to Hildy. "Don't you, ma'am?"

"Yets, yets, a pissician."

"Are you ailing, little missy?"

"Nod I. Dis total stranger neggs to me." She took three careful steps back.

The gassed and unconscious Whispering Wolfbanger sank to the polished teakwood floor of the cage.

"Heart attack," said the cowboy.

"Yets, I fear zo," agreed Hildy.

 **6**

The Chinese neopath smiled contentedly. "This was the wisest move we ever made, Alice," he told his wife as they strolled through the underground park at Hidden Acres Estates. "Expensive, granted, to buy us a condo here, yet even so. . . ." He gave out a peaceful sigh.

"You certainly do seem much more relaxed, Sun Yen. I'd begun to worry about you back when—"

"Your worries are over."

The park, which was forty-six feet below ground, was bathed in a never ending afternoon sunlight. The stately trees, neat lawns and pathways, the rustic benches all seemed to give off a pleasant glow.

"The cost," admitted Alice, "is high, but so long as you're happy, it doesn't matter."

"Not just happy, my dear, but secure. I know that down here beneath Greater Los Angeles we are ... Yikes!" He gave a sudden leap up into the mild air.

Then, letting go of his wife's arm, he went galloping across a patch of green lawn and dived down behind a bench.

His puzzled wife hurried over to him. "Whatever is wrong, Sun Yen?"

"Him! Him!" He raised up, so that part of his head showed above the bench back, and pointed nervously at a lanky figure who was striding along one of the sylvan paths. "He's here!"

Squinting, his wife looked toward the distant figure. "He does look something like Jake Pace, doesn't he?"

"It's Pace! It's Pace. The man's here, here in our idyllic Hidden Acres," mumbled Sun Yen. "He's a harbinger of trouble and devastation. Over the years, Alice, every time we've been anywhere near him, violence has ensued. Explosions, donnybrooks, assorted mayhem and—"

"He's probably only visiting a friend."

"Men like him, ruthless private investigators, have no friends. They're all loners who ... Look! Look! He's wearing a Realty Box clipped to his lapel. God, Pace and his leggy, trouble-prone wife are no doubt intending to move here. We'd better pack our—"

"You have to relax. Strive to recapture the mood you had only moments ago."

"Suppose we end up with Odd Jobs, Inc. as our next-door neighbors."

Unaware of the anxiety he was sowing, Jake continued on his way. "Interesting," he told the voxbox on his lapel.

"Each tree is a meticulously rendered replica of a real tree, such as you might find growing above ground," the realty box explained as Jake moved across the park. "And just sniff the air, Mr. Paloma. Mixed right here in our own plant, without a drop of smog in it. Heated, each and every day, to the always welcome temp of sixty-eight degrees."

"Marvelous. Now what about the suite I inquired about?"

"Awk . . . awk . . . negative reading . . . awk . . . Beg pardon, sir. You were saying?"

"I heard the Kirkyard suite was among those I might consider buying."

"Step through that latticework archway yonder and stop upon the magenta rectangle, won't you, please," instructed the box. "I fear, sir, you were misinformed."

"The young lady did die last week, didn't she?" persisted Jake.

"Through no fault of ours."

Jake halted on the designated rectangle. "The point being, she is no longer residing in—"

"Down, please."

The rectangle flapped down, Jake dropped onto a padded slide. He went shooting down and around until he popped through a swinging portal to find himself standing in a corridor. The corridor had been designed to resemble a stretch of spring woodlands. Only the brass doorknobs and the wall lamps spoiled the effect.

"Can we at least take a look at the Kirkyard—?"

"Mr. Paloma . . . Is that a Hungarian name, by the way?"

"Only partially," replied Jake. "If we could see the—"

"The Kirkyard family, so I am informed, has not decided what they will do with the—"

"Would it hurt to take a gander? Then I could maybe approach the grieving relatives myself and persuade—"

"Awk . . . awk . . . negative . . . Excuse me, sir. I was just contacting the Management Center," explained the box on his lapel. "They inform me that visiting the suite is quite impossible. However, I'm happy to say that on this selfsame floor we have a comparable vacancy which—"

"I'll have, I guess, to settle for that." Grinning, Jake dropped his hand into his trouser pocket.

The object he extracted looked something like

a fat silver key. He touched it to the base of the box.

"Awk . . . Bawk!" The voxbox rattled, shuddered, puffed out a single puff of bluish smoke. "I am now at your command, sahib. Do with me what you will."

After dropping the control rod away in his pocket, Jake suggested, "Take me to the Kirkyard suite."

"To hear is to obey. To the left, the sixth door over, sir, between the two sturdy oak trees."

Jake moved along the thick green sward, reached between the tree trunks and caught hold of the doorknob. "Locked."

"Forgive me, effendi. I'll buzz it open."

Bbbbizzzzzz!

The knob hummed, clicked and then turned freely in Jake's hand. He pushed and a section of brush swung inward.

"There's a step down going in," cautioned the helpful box.

 **7**

Neon-trimmed sailboats were racing far out on the night Pacific. From his glazed-in balcony Jake could see a dozen triangles of colored light gliding across the clear night. He had a suite on the thirteenth floor of the Malibu-Ritz Hotel, which was built on a massive stilt-foundation in the surf. At six minutes beyond nine he punched out a special number on the tapproof pixphone he'd placed on the neotile table next to his sling chair.

Seconds later Hildy, seated in the driveseat of her skycar, appeared on the screen. "Wellsir, that's one thing I can quit worrying about," she said, smiling. "You're still among the living."

"My current policy is to continue in that

mode for an indefinite period. Wither are you bound?"

His wife replied, "Manhattan."

"Why?"

"As planned, I got into Secretary Tintin's suite at the Whoopee Arms and—"

"Disguised as Baroness Eed?"

Hildy touched at the close-cropped dark wig she was now wearing. "I'm somebody else now," she explained. "Details upcoming."

"You look a mite dowdy."

"Proving once again that I'm a mistress of disguise. Quit heckling and listen, will you."

"Continue."

"Tintin was out and the two Secret Service agents watching his digs weren't especially formidable," Hildy reported. "I used a hypnomist on them. When they awaken, they'll remember me as being three chunky ladies from a new feminist terror group. Once inside the place . . . and, Jake, he's got it all furnished in black leather and torture implements . . . once inside I dug into his pixphone records and . . . Hold on, I'll show you some of what I copied."

Jake's phone screen lost Hildy's image, was filled with pulsating purple light and then gave him a picture of a husky blonde young woman.

"Banana oil," the blonde said in a lush voice.

"Ulp," a male voice was heard to say.

As with most pixphone tapes, you heard both sides of the conversation but saw only the caller.

"Are you ready, Lloyd honey, for your instructions?"

"I—am—ready."

The contract for the construction of sixteen new White Slave Discount Whorehouses is to be awarded to the Acme Building Corp of East Moline, Illinois. See to it."

"I—shall—see—to—it."

"Dandy. Bye, love."

More purple light, then Hildy reappeared. "There are four other conversations of a similar nature with her over the past month," she said. "Recognize the lady?"

"She looks moderately familiar, but—"

"And you claim to be the show business maven in the family. Dimwit, that's Amazon Brodsky, star of the world's most popular satnet soap opera, *Wretched Mess*."

"Soap opera isn't show business," Jake maintained. "She's on the list our late client provided us."

"Yes, along with the US Secretary of Vice and four other notables here and abroad," replied Hildy. "Folks Sylvie Kirkyard's convinced are mind-controlled by someone within Brainz, Inc."

"Secretary Tintin sure seems to be. Did Amazon put him into a trance with that trigger word on each call?"

"She did. And it might be a trick she learned maybe from Dr. Death?"

Nodding, Jake said, "She didn't look to be in a trance herself. That might indicate she's a bit higher in the organization than he is."

"Which is why I'm on my way to Manhattan, where Amazon has a townhouse."

Hildy sighed a small sigh. "Out of touch with the popular arts, woefully ignorant when it comes to key figures in the academic world."

"Ah, I've got it," he said. "You're Professor Zuleika Paternoster of Kansas Pop College. Consulting editor of *The Scholarly Journal for the Appreciation of Mass Market Trash*."

"Very good," said his wife. "I'm going to do an essay on *Veiled Incest in the Image Projection of Amazon Brodsky*. I've already set up an interview with her for tomorrow."

"That article sounds like something I'd just love to curl up with on a chill evening before the fire," Jake said. "Be careful. She seems like a tough lady."

"As am I," Hildy reminded. "What've you come up with?"

"Sylvie Kirkyard was murdered."

"Oh, so?"

"A gas called Asthmaline was used," he

continued. "I found traces of the stuff in the aircirc outlets in her suite."

"What is the stuff?"

"Eh? Are you admitting to being ill informed in the area of chemical-biological weaponry? For shame."

Hildy shook her head. "Ego feel better now?"

"We're just about even, yes. Anyway, my love, Dr. Death invented this particular asphyxiating gas a few years back," he told her. "One of the things it does is cause its victims to take on an orange tint in the hours immediately following death. When I heard Sylvie's skin was orangish, I figured—"

"Whoa now. Where'd you find that out? None of the accounts I—"

"All the original reports of her death were suppressed. Law Force, Murder Squad, medics."

"But you got hold of the originals?"

"And the fakes as well, with the help of Steranko the—"

"Ugh. I really wish we didn't have to work with that abominable little skinhead."

"Funny, he always speaks highly of you."

"No doubt. What else have you found out? Do you know who introduced the gas into her rooms?"

"Not yet," Jake admitted. "I do know, though, that a good deal of effort's gone into covering up the truth about what happened to her. The law and medical folks were bribed or otherwise silenced. Bribes must've been given out at Hidden Acres Estates, too, to allow access to her apartment and the aircirc system."

"Don't the visitor tapes show who's been—"

"They well might, if they hadn't, quite accidently I'm told, been erased. For all the suites on that floor," said Jake. "There are no records of who visited that level for the three weeks prior to her death or for the night of her death either."

"That makes things a little more difficult."

"A little, yes," agreed Jake.

"What next?"

"I'm going to look over her two alleged friends, Oscar McCracklin and Dr. Rose Sanhamel," he answered. "I want some information on what went on, hither and yon, during those three missing weeks. I think—"

Thump!

"Jake? What is it?"

Thump! Karump!

"I have a visitor."

A sandy-haired man was dangling, upside down by one foot, outside against the balcony dome. He wore a dark blue one-piece worksuit and was tangled up with a length of nylocord. The other end of the rope was apparently attached to the roof of the Malibu-Ritz.

"Trouble?" asked Hildy, concerned.

"He looks to be having some," said Jake. "Where're you staying in Manhattan?"

"The Seuling-Plaza. I'll be there in a half hour or so."

"Okay, I'll phone you in an hour."

"Fine, but ... Well, okay." The phone screen went blank.

Leaving his chair, Jake walked over to take a closer look at the dangling man.

"I hate to take aid and comfort from the enemy," said the sandy-haired visitor as Jake hauled him in out of the night through a sliding panel in the glaz dome.

"The rule is you're not supposed to give aid and comfort to the enemy," Jake pointed out, untangling the nylocord from around his ankle. "Taking it is oaky doaks. You'd be Bert Higby?"

"Well ... yes," the middle-sized artist conceded. "I was ... sneaking up on you, Mr. Pace."

"Much like SplatterMan?"

Higby looked down at his black sneakers. "It's easier to draw than do."

"Sit," suggested Jake.

Higby held out his arms. "I better point out that, unlike my graphic novel hero, I don't carry much in the way of weapons."

"Found that out when I was helping you in.

Only this second-rate stungun." Jake held it up by its barrel tip.

The artist slapped at his left armpit. "How'd you do that?"

"It's called frisking."

"Yes, but I didn't even notice."

"Exactly. Sit yourself, Higby," Jake invited, a thin grin on his face. "Then explain how you come to know I'm here."

Higby sat in a candy-striped rumphugger chair. "The answer to that is easy," he said while massaging his right knee. "I followed you."

"From where?"

"Sylvie's place."

"Where the hell were you?"

"Lurking in the brush in the corridor. I'm much better at that than I am at shinnying ropes."

"Apparently." Jake returned to his chair. "Why were you lurking at Hidden Acres?"

"Trying to find out who killed Sylvie."

"You don't believe her death was accidental."

"It wasn't," Higby stated. "And the fact that a prestigious, and damn expensive, agency like Odd Jobs, Inc. has been hired to wipe out any last traces of—"

"Hey, whoa," cut in Jake, angry. "We *solve* mysteries, we don't tamper with evidence or cover up the—"

"So you say. Yet my research into how the average detective agency functions leads me to ... I do a lot of research for my SplatterMan novels so—"

"Odd Jobs, Inc. doesn't happen to be your average agency, Higby."

"So you say. Just the—"

"Tell me how come you think she was murdered."

Higby rubbed his fingertips over his knee, glanced out at the darkness he'd recently been dangling in. "Would you tell me who hired you?"

"Nope."

"Is it Dr. Sanhamel?"

Jake gave a negative shake of his head. "Why should she—"

"One of Sylvie's damn brothers?"

Jake leaned forward. "Look, Higby, my wife and I were hired by someone who also thinks Sylvie Kirkyard was murdered."

"Who'd care a damn about that besides me? Most of the other guys she was seeing don't much care for—"

"When was the last time you saw Sylvie?"

"Up close, a week before ... before she died."

"And how many times in the two weeks before that?"

"We had three dates," he replied. "See, she

was devoting a good bit of her time to . . . well, to something she was devoting her time to."

"Digging into things she suspected were wrong at Brainz, Inc.?"

Higby blinked. "Well, yes. But how'd you—"

"Where does Dr. Sanhamel come in?"

"For one thing she was watching Sylvie's suite."

"Watching how?"

"Lurking in the brush, like me."

"This was going on before Sylvie died?"

"I was worried," answered the artist. "Sylvie'd told me some of what she was concerned about. I felt whoever was using Brainz, Inc. for his own ends might just try to hurt her."

"So maybe Dr. Sanhamel had the same notion you did."

"I don't think so, Mr. Pace. I trailed her on a few occasions . . . I'm fairly proficient at tracking, so long as it doesn't involve heights and ropes."

"Trailed her where?"

"She had clandestine meetings with Dr. Death."

"They're colleagues."

"Then why not meet at one of the Kirktronics office complexes? Instead, they rendezvoused at a White Slave Discount Whorehouse in the Santa Monica Sector."

"That could've been business."

"It wasn't, I'm certain," said the artist. "Kirktronics has no overt business links with that chain of bordellos. And, in case you're going to suggest this next, neither Rose Sanhamel nor Dr. Death are the sort of people to patronize a place like that."

Narrowing his left eye, Jake looked upward. The night sky was rich with stars and skycars. "Sylvie and Dr. Sanhamel were friends."

"Sylvie may've thought so, but I never trusted that lady."

"Anyone else hanging around Sylvie's?"

"Not that I spotted."

"Were you there the night she died?"

"No, I wasn't." He shook his head forlornly. "If I had been, she might be alive. I had a deadline I couldn't miss on my newest Splatter-Man graphic novel. The final book in the *Too Late The Disemboweler* trilogy. So I was at my board that . . ." He brought his hand up to his eyes and began to cry softly.

Jake asked him, "Besides Dr. Sanhamel and Dr. Death, who else do you think's involved?"

"All of them." He sniffed, wiped at his nose with the back of his hand. "Her brothers, all of her other relatives. A rotten bunch. Sylvie . . . she was completely different from any of them."

"Both her brothers?"

"Louts and scoundrels, the pair."

"She had another close friend at Brainz, Inc. Fellow named Oscar—"

"Oscar McCracklin," said Higby. "On the surface he seems amiable enough, but . . . I don't know, I've never quite trusted the guy."

"Could be you're jealous of him."

"Oscar McCracklin? He's an old man, over fifty. No, I simply didn't like to see Sylvie put so much faith and trust in McCracklin."

Jake sat back. "I don't know how long I'm going to be in CalSouth," he said. "I'd appreciate it if you ceased working in my vicinity or staging these little commando raids. Okay?"

Sniffling once more, the artist asked, "You really are working to find out who killed her?"

"I am, yes."

"So you say," said Higby.

The lean young black man said, grinning amiably, "Hey, bitch, you ought to write a nurfing article about me."

Smoothing the short skirt of her gray neowool bizsuit, Hildy shifted in her glaz chair, swallowed nervously and said, "That's an idea, except I have no idea who you are."

His eyes widened, his eyebrows quivered. "You mammyjammers hear what this nurfing bitch say?" he asked of the six young men who stood around his chair in the greenroom of the satnet studios in Manhattan. "She know don't who the nurf I am."

"Are you somebody?" Hildy inquired.

"You mammyjammers hear that? This mammyjamming bitch want to know is I a nurfing somebody. Nurfin A, lady, I am Barf McBernie."

After a few seconds Hildy responded with, "Oh?"

"Barf McBernie," he repeated, watching her face. "You know, bitch, also known as the 'Funniest Man in the Universe.' "

"A comedian, are you?"

McBernie laughed. "This mammyjamming bitch want to know am I a comedian."

The six hangerson chuckled, rolled their eyes, nudged each other. Three of them were black, two were white, the other Chinese.

Hildy said, "Pleased to meet you, Mr. McBernie, anyway. I'm Dr. Zuleika Paternoster of—"

"Zuleika?" McBernie bounced twice on his plaz slingchair. "Her mammyjamming name is Zuleika. You mammyjammers hear what her name is? Zuleika. That's funny. That is one mammyjamming funny name."

"It's not as lyrical as Barf I admit, yet—"

"Hey, bitch. You trying to jump wise with me?"

"Beg pardon?" she asked, feigning puzzlement. Barf McBernie's name was also on the list of mind-controlled people their client had provided them. Hildy was curious as to why he was here at this taping session for Amazon

Brodsky's satnet soap opera. "Have I offended you in some—"

"No nurfing around now, bitch. You really never heard of me?"

"I'm afraid not, Mr. McBernie. You see, being involved in my own area of popular culture I—"

"My mammyjamming vidcaz albums. Ain't you never seen one?"

"Well, I may have. I don't actually, though, recall—"

"You mammyjammers hear what this bitch say? She never saw my album entitled—— Your——. You sure, bitch?"

"Well, perhaps if you told me what it was about."

"About?" He bounced thrice.

"The theme, plot, the nuances of—"

"Crap, lady, it were just funny. I mean, seventeen million mammyjamming people bought the nurfing thing."

"Congratulations."

"I did, you know, my whackin' off routine. The faggot impersonations. You never saw it?"

"Doesn't sound familiar. Chiefly I watch soap operas and—"

"How about my next vidcaz. That was called I——Her——. You saw that, didn't you, bitch?"

Hildy considered. "No, I don't really think so. But possibly—"

"What about my newest one? I mean, twenty-six million nurfing mammyjammers have done bought that in the past two weeks, you know."

"What's it called?"

"——— ———, ———." McBernie eyed her hopefully.

"No, I'm afraid not, though it sounds like it must be fun." She fished a notebook and electripencil from out her shoulderbag. "——— ———, ———, was it? I'll make a note to be on the lookout."

Standing up, McBernie scowled around at his entourage. "You mammyjammers been hearing all this? I'm supposed to be the funniest mammyjamming comedian in this whole nurfing universe and this bitch, she don't even know who I is. Shit." He sat down, bounced twice, folded his arms.

"Why exactly are you here at the satnet studios, Mr. McBernie?" asked Hildy.

"Crap, oh dear, don't you even know that?"

"No, which is why—"

"I'm going to do a mammyjamming cameo on this *Wretched Mess* soaper. I play a patient in the nurfing Long Island Hospital for the Disgustingly Rich. This bitch Amazon Brodsky's also a patient there."

"Sounds most interesting."

"Of course it's interesting, bitch. I mean, here you got the funniest man on the face of the mammyjamming earth and he's going to be on the world's most successful nurfing soaper. Shit, that's bound to set off sparks."

Hildy smiled her academic smile. "My, then I picked an excellent day to visit, didn't I?"

"An excellent mammyjamming day? Crap, bitch, how many days you get to see somebody as important as me up this close, huh?"

"Not many," Hildy admitted.

"Nurfing A right."

A green door slid silently open in the left-hand wall. "Um ... Mr. McBernie," said the small freckled man who had appeared on the threshold. "We're going to commence taping in about ten minutes. Would you come down to the set now, please."

"Who am I?" he rose up, pointing at the man.

"Hum?"

"Who am I?"

"Oh, god, don't tell me you've got amnesia."

"Just tell this bitch who I am."

"Barf McBernie," said the soap opera assistant director. "Does that ring a bell at—"

"Crap, I know who I am, nurfhead. I want you to tell this lady here how important I is."

"Oh, yes," the little freckled director said. "He's important."

"Bitch never heard of me."

"Really? That's astonishing."

"You bet your nurfing ass it is. She never even saw —— ——, ——."

The freckled man gave Hildy a pitying look. "But, goodness, it's number two on the Manhattan *Times* list of vidcaz hits."

"I'm sorry," said Hildy.

McBernie moved slowly for the doorway. "Crap, I thought everybody heard of me."

One of his followers patted him on the back.

After McBernie and his circle had gone the freckled director said to Hildy, "I do hope you haven't upset him too much, Dr. Paternoster. He's playing a key role in the next few episodes of *Wretched Mess*."

"Comedians are noted for laughing through their tears," Hildy pointed out.

"I suppose so, yes. Well, Miss Brodsky will be able to chat with you soon as she's finished this morning's taping."

"Thank you," said Hildy.

When she was alone she wrote Barf McBernie's name in her notebook, put a question mark after it.

The monitor on the far wall of the green room showed a medium longshot of a luxurious glaz and metal medical complex.

"... bring you Book 26, Chapter 11 of the

heartwarming story, *Wretched Mess*, the only soap opera in the history of broadcasting to win a Nobel prize," an unseen deep-voiced announcer was intoning. "As you may remember, beautiful young Rachel Oz learned only moments ago that she is suffering from Malzberg's Syndrome, that dread disease that causes increasing lugubriousness in its helpless victims. Only one doctor on the face of the earth has ever been able to cure the malady and that is none other than Lex Shootry, MD, the handsome and debonair playboy surgeon whom Rachel elbowed in the ribs at the recent Tax Shelter Millionaires' Ball in Majorca. Will he overcome his pique and try to save Rachel's young life? And what of the famed shockrock singer, Blind 'Lectric Kadillac, whom Rachel's madcap father, old Wildcat Oz, one-time softball pitcher, ran down while flying too low in a stolen skycar? Will Blind 'Lectric regain the will to live? And what of Wildcat Oz' strange and unnatural urges toward his lovely daughter? How can . . ."

Very quietly, Hildy left her chair and eased to the doorway. She touched the out panel and the door slid open.

The set in use was an illuminated rectangle some hundred yards away. Between the mock hospital room and Hildy was mostly darkness. Entering it, she headed for Amazon Brodsky's dressing room.

Amazon portrayed the trouble-prone Rachel Oz and was out on the set right now, strapped to a thermobed. A kindly old physician was examining her.

". . . how do you feel, my child?"

"Lugubrious, Dr. Shestack."

"Ah, just as I feared."

Moving over cables and wires, Hildy reached the star's dressing room. The sliding door was an inch or so open. Hildy stood listening.

Then she got the door to open wider and stepped into the room. The silvery walls were thick with framed photos, mostly of the handsome Amazon Brodsky accepting assorted awards and trophies.

Sitting upright in a gold-plated chair was Barf McBernie. He was staring straight ahead, arms stiff at his sides.

"Are you okay, young man?" asked Hildy.

"I–await–my–orders," he answered, not looking at her, not moving at all.

"Orders from whom?"

"I–await–my–orders."

Hildy took a few steps toward the entranced comedian. "Guess it's no use asking anymore foolish questions."

"I–await–my–orders."

"Okay, I'll just browse around while you're awaiting." Hildy crossed to the dressing table.

She was examining the scatter of stuff atop it

when the door to the dressing room opened wide. In the mirror she saw two large men in white medsuits and surgical masks enter.

Turning, smiling innocently, she reached into her shoulderbag. Her fingers grabbed the handle of her stungun. "Shouldn't you fellows be out on the set?"

"Oh," the larger of the two told her, "we're not actors."

Jake crouched slightly before the bathchamber mirror. "Perfect," he told himself, giving his false moustache a final, careful pat. Straightening up, he did a slow turn. The one-piece sky-blue worksuit he was wearing fit perfectly. "The show world lost a brilliant—"

The hotel phone in the living room was buzzing.

Jake trotted in, flipped the answer toggle. He kept his side of the conversation visually blank. "Yeah?"

A plump, bald man of fifty some was on the screen, looking nervous and anxious. "Mr. Pace?"

This, juding from photos he'd studied before

heading westward, was Oscar McCracklin, the Brainz, Inc. tech who'd built Sylvie's simulacrum for her and installed the mindspot. "Who's calling?"

McCracklin glanced to his left, to his right. "Tell him we have a mutual friend," he said. "And that she . . . that this mutual friend phoned me this morning."

"Holy crow," muttered Jake. "And told you about me, McCracklin?"

"Is that you, Pace?"

"She gave you my name, told you where I was staying?" Jake had informed Moneyback Smith, who was storing Sylvie at the safehouse in Wisconsin, where he was. In case an emergency came up. Smith, the halfwit, must've told Sylvie.

"Is that you, Pace? I hate to blurt out—"

"Where are you phoning from?"

"My home, but—"

"Hang up. I'll call you back on a tap-proof phone."

"Well . . . My number is—"

"I've got that. Hang up."

"But it's unlist—"

"Nevertheless." Jake broke the connection, went striding to the tap-proof pixphone out on the domed balcony.

The Pacific had a blurred, hazy look this morning.

Jake punched out the number he wanted.

McCracklin looked even more uneasy on this screen. "Is Pace there?"

"I'm Pace."

"You look like some sort of repairman who—"

"It's a god damn disguise. Now what in the hell do you—"

"Do private investigators put on a disguise just to make a call to—"

"Sylvie told me this morning that you were working for her, you and your wife. And she mentioned where you were staying."

"So?"

"First tell me if you've confirmed her suspicions. Was she actually murd—"

"We report only to our client."

"But, surely, since Sylvie told me how to reach you, you must—"

"Right now all I know is that you say she told you about me," said Jake.

McCracklin coughed into his hand. "You know about the three missing weeks?"

"Yep."

"Since she left, the past couple of days I've been doing some further investigating myself," said McCracklin. "I can fill you in, I think, on some of the blanks in the android's mindspot."

"Have you told Sylvie what you found out?"

"She suggested I tell you first."

"Okay, tell me."

"I can't now," he said, looking off screen. "Can you come to my home in, say, an hour?"

"Nope. How about four this afternoon?"

McCracklin frowned. "I'm due to make a speech then," he said. "Perhaps, though, you could meet me there."

"Where?"

"In Oxnard."

"Oxnard?"

"I'm speaking at the Write Festival, being held at the Sports & Literature Drome there. Don't know if you'll care for my talk, but afterwards we—"

"See you at four." Jake hung up, gave his moustache another pat and hurried out of the suite.

The pimp had neon teeth, electric hair and a two-piece yellow funsuit. He stood, wide-legged, on the cracked plaz sidewalk in front of the White Slave Discount Whorehouse, hectoring and cajoling the midday passersby. His perennial smile flashed in the basic colors of the light spectrum, his foot-long blond hair stood straight up, crackling and dancing. His six brass buttons piped, "low low prices ... unbeatable deals ... poontang at poor man's prices ..."

Jake parked his landvan partially on the crumbling curb, stumbled getting free of the cab, went shuffling over to the sidewalk pimp. "This the Santa Monica Sector White Slave Discount Warehouse?" he inquired in a numb voice, squinting at the slip of yellow faxpaper he was clutching in his grease-smeared left hand. "Are you Mr. Bascofigli?"

"Whorehouse, daddy," corrected the pimp.

"Hum?"

"This here is the White Slave Discount WHOREHOUSE, my man. One of over 1900 such establishments across this promised land of ours, serving man's basic need for nubile nookie at prices all can afford."

"Warehouse, whorehouse," said the impatient Jake, "are you Bascofigli?"

"Does it seem logical to you that the Associate Manager of this pleasure palace would be standing out in the noonday sun sweating his toke off?" The pimp's hair sizzle and swayed, his buttons chirped, "Low-cost lewdness . . . vile perversions or naughty normalcy . . ."

"I got an order," explained Jake as he fluttered the paper in his hand, "to check out a malfunction in your data system."

"My data system is just fine, daddy." The pimp's grin throbbed blue, green, yellow, red.

"Where's Mr. Bascofigli?"

"Who knows?" The pimp shrugged, then noticed two skytruckers climbing out of their freshly landed producecraft. "This is the place, lads. The White Slave Discount Whorehouse has prices so low that you'll think we're all insane and bonkers hereabouts. That's right, gents, you'll flip your flapper and pop your peepers when you gander our low, low prices. No frills don't mean no thrills!"

"How much," inquired the larger of the two truckers, "for a virgin Armenian girl of sixteen?"

The pimp's electric hair wiggled and waved while he considered the inquiry. His buttons babbled, ". . . we cut costs, not your fun . . . try our on-the-bare-boards special . . ."

"Listen, we do have a sixteen-year-old Armenian girl," the pimp informed the skytrucker with a glowing grin. "Thing is, daddy, she's no longer a virgin." He consulted his platinum and ruby tokwatch. "Gee, if you'd gotten here just forty-five minutes ago, you could've been numero uno."

The second trucker suggested, "What say we try someplace else, Leslie?"

"Well, I don't know, Elmore. I sort of got my heart set on a sixteen—"

"I'll go on in," said Jake and went shuffling on in through the revolving door.

An enormous high-ceilinged room stretched out in front of him. There were about fifty aircots arranged in fuzzy rows, each not quite shielded by an opaque plaz screen. You could see bits and pieces of naked young women and anxious, hurried customers. Hear cries, screams and whispers of joy, real and feigned. Floating high above it all was a huge six-faced digital clock.

"What's your pleasure, hon?" asked a plump woman seated behind an old-fashioned cash register.

Jake consulted his faxpaper. "Mr. Bascofigli?"

Scowling, the woman jerked a thumb ceilingward. "Fag Floor's upstairs, junior."

Jake made a grumbling noise in his throat. "Listen, lady, I'm no fruitbar," he told her. "Nor am I the kind of guy who has to buy his romance."

"Anybody, hon, with a droopy moustache like yours sure ain't going to get any free."

"Be that as it may, I work for Data Doctor. We fix your data systems, computers, even small household servomechs."

"Do you want some nookie or not?"

"I want to get into your basement."

"Just a minute now."

He held out the paper. "You got some kind of malfunction down there, lady."

"Hold on, hold on." She pushed a button and the cash register drawer came whizzing open. Feeling around in one of the tiny compartments, she located a tiny tin box. "Let me pop in my contacts, lover, and read that damn thing."

"How come you don't wear the things all the time?"

"Because, if it's any of your damn business, they dim the natural sparkle of my eyes." After inserting the lenses, she snatched the paper from him and read it slowly and carefully. "Nobody told me about this."

"They told me," Jake said. "And, listen, lady, my time is just as valuable as yours, you know. I mean to say, I got three more data storage systems to check out before nightfall and it's already—"

"Okay, spare me your sad story." She tossed the sheet back at him. "Go on down and do what you will."

"I ought to see Mr. Bascofigli first."

"He's up in Oxnard."

"Oxnard?"

"Go on down there, junior, and get fixing."

"Just trying to do my damn job." Giving her a curt nod, Jake headed for the downramp.

 **10**

Two skycars collided in the murky early afternoon air outside his balcony. Amid thumps,
the rending of metal and plaz, yells and horn-
hooting, the drivers and passengers were auto-
matically ejected. A tanned girl in a neosilk
bikinisuit came whizzing through the fuzzy sky
to bonk against Jake's glaz balcony dome. Arms
flapping, legs kicking, she bounced on it twice
before her airbelt started functioning. Then she
went floating away.

Jake seated himself again at his tapproof
pixphone and punched out the number of
Hildy's Manhattan hotel.

Still no answer.

"Checking out Amazon Brodsky shouldn't have taken her this—"

The phone rang while he was still resting his hand on it.

"Yeah?"

Sylvie Kirkyard showed on the screen. "I hadn't heard anything from—"

"You weren't supposed to communicate with anyone," he told his client.

The survivors of the midair crash were still bobbing around outside, sustained by their airbelts.

"Certainly I can phone my own private investigator to inquire how his probing into the circumstances surrounding my very own death is—"

"Who gave you this number?"

"Why, Mr. Smith. He said you'd given it to him in case—"

"In case of an emergency, which this isn't," he told her evenly. "And even if calling me does seem like one to you, Sylvie, pixing Oscar McCracklin sure as hell doesn't qualify as—"

"But I haven't called Oscar," said the blond android. "After all, Mr. Pace, I am not the typical scatter-brained heiress you apparently—"

"Whoa, wait," he urged. "You haven't been in touch with McCracklin?"

"Of course not. What makes you think I have?"

"McCracklin," replied Jake. "He phoned earlier, claimed you'd told him I was out here working for you"

She shook her head. "I didn't. That has to mean—"

"I'll find out what it means when I keep my four o'clock appointment at the Write Festival with him."

"You oughtn't to do that, since it's quite obviously a trap of some sort."

"Exactly."

"I don't quite under—"

"Never mind. How well did you know—"

"Could you try not to use the past tense with me so much. I find it unsettling. I know I'm dead, but even so. . . ."

"How well *do* you know Wallace Wind?"

"Not very," she answered. "No one does really, since he's very near to being a recluse. His Total Enterprises has tried to buy us out several times, but Kirktronics has been able to hold off . . . surely he isn't behind this?"

Jake told her, "It's the other way round probably."

"What do you—"

"In a little less than two weeks he's having Dr. Death and Dr. Sanhamel call on him at one of his many estates, the Mojave one," he said. "Because Wind doesn't cotton to mingling, and because he's one of the richest and most powerful gents in the world, they're going to have his initial mindspot session at his place instead of theirs."

"Wallace Wind? But that's dreadful," gasped Sylvie. "Why, Total Enterprises controls about 26 percent of everything on Earth. Business, banking, pro sports, entertainment. If they can take him over, why, they'll be even closer to running everything."

"Yep, that's exactly the way they see it," he said. "Which is probably why you were killed."

She touched her cheek. "I am right then. I was murdered?"

"You were," he said and gave a quick account of how it'd been done.

She was quiet for a few seconds after he finished. "You don't know who?"

"Not yet."

"And how does the taking over of Wallace Wind fit in?"

"Dr. Sanhamel and Dr. Death have been having clandestine getogethers at the Santa Monica Sector White Slave Discount Whorehouse, a chain Death owns a controlling interest in and—"

"I didn't know that."

"A siphoning friend of mine unearthed that news," said Jake. "To continue. Two days before you died you found out about their meetings. You trailed them there and, using one of your own Kirktronics eavesdrop guns, you listened to what they were saying in a secret meeting room up on the Fag Floor."

"I did? I have no recolection of doing that at all." Sylvie rubbed her fingertips slowly across her temple. "Well, of course, my memory ends before that, so I couldn't."

"The two docs discovered you'd overheard, that you were planning to warn Wallace Wind," he said. "Seems likely, though I don't as yet have proof, that that's the reason for your murder."

Sylvie said, "But Rose Sanhamel had been a friend of mine since I was a child. She made the mindspot for—"

"Did she know it was going into an andy replica of you?"

"Oscar and I decided not to tell her," the android replied. "What he actually inserted in my skull was a dupe of the mindspot Rose made."

Nodding, Jake said, "She hasn't been on your side for quite a while."

"Are you certain? Since you're an ace investigator, I suppose you must be. Yet I find it difficult to believe Rose could—"

"I spent my morning in the bowels of the Whorehouse," he said. "It's their policy to keep tapes of whatever goes on in every room. Dr. Death and Dr. Sanhamel forgot about that. I found the vidtapes of several of their meetings down there. I can play you copies I—"

"I don't think I wish to hear those or see them. Not just yet," she said. "Do you also know . . . which of my brothers, Kevin or Ross, is in cahoots with them?"

"That I haven't determined. The good doctors mentioned neither of your brothers in their chats."

"Perhaps that's a good sign."

"Don't count on anything being a good sign in this mess," Jake advised.

"What will you do next? Do you really think it's wise to walk headlong into a possible trap that's been—"

"I never walk into anything headlong," Jake said and hung up.

He tried to reach Hildy once again and got no answer.

 **11**

Hildy's nose quivered before she opened her eyes. "Scotch broth?" she murmured.

"I'm very much afraid it is," said a voice nearby. "Yesterday it was Bulgarian cucumber soup and the day before consommé Brunoise. The worst thus far, in the five days I've been here, was Portuguese whale—"

"Hold off," requested Hildy. She'd opened her eyes now and discovered she was flat on her back in a chill pea-green room. Flat on her back, double-strapped to a floatcot.

"We're in the Incorrigibles Ward. In case you were planning next to inquire were you were."

"That was, yes, one of the questions I was mulling around in my somewhat fuzzy head."

She turned, as best she could, to take in the occupant of the cot next to hers.

"That's all a dodge, of course." He was a chubby blond man, his cherubic face speckled with stubble. He, too, was held down with plaz straps. "You're no more incorrigible than I, Mrs. Pace."

Hildy blinked. "What makes you think I'm—"

"They took off your disguise after they brought you in. Naturally I recognized one of the most famous distaff ops in the nation," he said. "Were you involved with Wallace Wind, too? He didn't mention Odd Jobs, Inc. the last time I talked to him, but since he's a cagey old coot it's—"

"This ward we're sharing," she cut in. "Where exactly is it?"

"Oh, sorry. I thought you knew. This is Bum Reservation number three, in the Bowery Zone of Manhattan," explained her roommate. "This wing, which is over the Koch Memorial Soup Kitchen, we have all to ourselves. The pungent odors wafting up from—"

"And who the heck are you?"

"Forgive me for not introducing myself earlier," he said with an apologetic smile. "I'm Sheldon Sickmann. Perhaps you've heard of—"

"The only Sickmann I've heard of is Senior Vice President in Charge of New Accounts at the Krankheit, Sygdom, Machalam, Ugonjwa and Sickmann advertising agency here in Manhattan."

Sickmann chuckled. "That's me. I'm flattered you—"

"I keep up with the minutiae of the business world. How long have I been here?"

"Approximately three hours," he replied. "That's an estimate, since with my wrist watch strapped to my side I can't—"

"Meaning they probably brought me here straight from the studios," she mused. "And used a low setting on their damn stunguns." By twisting to the right, she could see the room's single window, small and high up. Late afternoon sky showed.

"Would you happen to know who they are?" asked the advertising executive.

"Don't you?"

"While I have some notions, I've seen no one but the servobot who brings the meals . . . all the meals are soup, by the way . . . I've seen nobody since I was dumped here."

"You don't know who dumped you, Mr. Sickmann?"

"It's a slightly embarrassing story, but I'll tell it none the less. I was en route to call on Wallace Wind, who was spending the day at his Westchester Enclave estate and had summoned me," said Sickmann. "I hate to admit it . . . well, I was driving a landcar, since old

WW loathes the sight and sound of skycars and aircraft of any sort . . . Odd, when you realize the old duffer owns six airlines and four major skycar companies . . . I was driving along and happened to notice two young women attempting to repair their landvan at the side of the slotway. They were wearing those nudipantz the young people are so enamored of at the moment and . . . I found myself pulling up and jumping from my vehicle to offer assistance. I'd barely introduced myself and offered aid when one of them whipped out a stungun. I awoke here five . . . I'm nearly certain I've been keeping fair track of the passing time . . . five days ago."

"You don't know why?"

"I suspect, only suspect, mind you, since the feeding bot isn't very responsive to my queries, that they want to keep me out of the way for a while. Looking on the bright side, soup kitchen downstairs and all, it's better than being dead and gone."

"And why does anyone want you out of the way?"

Sickmann lowered his voice. "Wallace Wind owns a pharmaceutical company. Actually he owns dozens, but the one I mean is Bedlam Brothers, located in Tampa, Fla."

"The Bedlam Brothers, Ches and Wal. I've

seen the animated vidwall commercials your agency does for their NoSneez Hayfever Capsules."

"I wrote the one in which the nose waltzes with the hankie," said Sickmann, smiling modestly. "The point is, Mrs. Pace, Bedlam has come up with something truly new and—"

"Your commercials say that about all their stuff."

"This time, however, it's true." His voice dropped to a whisper. "Listen, some whiz kid in their R & D lab cooked this one up. They're calling it, tenatively, Kure. It'll come in pill, capsule, and elixir form."

Hildy asked, "What's it do?"

"You may find this hard to believe . . . I did myself, lord knows. They showed me data, printouts, vidtapings," he whispered excitedly. "They've been sitting on Kure for near to three years, not letting a blessed word leak out. Testing, making absolutely certain it really works." He turned his head until he was looking directly across at Hildy. "The damn stuff cures every major and minor disease known to man. Quickly, with no side effects."

"C'mon," scoffed Hildy.

"That was my initial reaction, Mrs. Pace," he said. "Now, though, there is absolutely no doubt in my mind. Kure can cure cancer, heart disease,

herpes, the common cold, Malzberg's Syndrome
... Hell, you name it. Leprosy? Sure. Jock itch?
You bet. Acne? Clears it up overnight." His
eyes narrowed. "Can you imagine what a terrific ad campaign Krankheit, Sygdom, Machalah,
Ugonjwa and Sickmann can come up with for a
surefire new product like that?"

"I can, yes."

"Wallace Wind is husbanding this one himself and I was on my way to discuss our pro-
posed teaser campaign ... we're planning to
launch Kure in the spring of '05 ... and I made
that foolish mistake of stopping. I suspect that
perhaps a rival agency is behind this. Word
must've leaked out and they're trying to steal
the account by keeping me under wraps."

Hildy asked him, "Have you ever had any
dealings with Brainz, Inc.?"

"Funny you should mention Brainz, Inc.,"
Sickmann answered. "Old WW's been arrang-
ing to have a copy of his brain made by them, a
mindspot they call it."

"Then they'll control Kure, too," she said.

"What's that?"

"I'm going to have to get out of this place."

"Don't think I'm being overly negative, ma'am,
but even a formidable operative such as yourself will have one heck of a time getting free of
these restraints."

"In my sophomore year at CalState I did a term paper on the life and work of Harry Houdini," Hildy said.

"That's interesting. Although I don't think I know who—"

"I got an A."

12

She caught Jake halfway across the third level of the Oxnard Sports & Literature Drome. A pretty young woman with electric silver blonde hair, wearing a two-piece foilsuit. She was dragging a frail ninety-two-year-old man along in her wake.

"Jake Pace!" She grabbed his arm with her free hand, fingers tightening around his elbow. "Jake Pace! How zappy!"

Her sudden onslaught caused him to stumble and nudge a poster vendor. "Oops," said Jake.

"Get your posters of your favorite write groups," said the black vendor. "We got them all, folks. The Grubs, the Hacks, the Poetasters.

All the hot novelist collectives. Get off my mammyjamming foot, nurfhead."

"Excuse it."

"You're spoiling my shine. You better buy this poster of the Blockbusters to make it up to me. Ten dollars, mailing tube included."

Before Jake could make his negative reply, the blonde had tugged him to another part of the crowd. "Jake Pace!" Her electric hair stood up higher on her lovely head, crackling. "This makes my afternoon!"

"Splendid. Now, miss, if you'll let loose, I'll continue on my way to the Harlan Ellison Room so that I can partake of a lecture on—"

"I'm Felony Fulsom!" she explained, hair subsiding.

Jake gave her a bleak grin. "Pleased to meet—"

"This old dear is Harry Bangs!" Felony gave the old man in tow a few shakes.

"Is there any place," he wheezed, "where I might sit down to—"

"He's my other big catch of the day!" said Felony. "And now you!"

Jake was eyeing the frail white-haired Bangs and his loosely fitting 1980s style suit. "Bangs the sci fi writer?"

"Please don't," gasped Bangs, "call it that. It's *science fiction* if—"

"Harry's one of the sci fi greats!" said Felony,

hair rising and flickering. "When I heard he was making a speech here I popped in my skyjalopy and zoomed—"

"Well, it's been pleasant chatting," Jake told her. "But now I—"

"But I need you, too, Pace! For the show!"

He'd started to pull free, but halted. "Show?"

"I'm Talent Coordinator for *Munchin' at Veggies*! It's the top-rated tradvid talkieshow on the Coastnet! Our ratings are absolutely zappy!"

". . . all these new groups in strange and bizarre attire," old H.Harry Bangs was muttering, seeming to sink further into his last-century suit. "Takes four or five of them to turn out one novel. Now in my heyday, back in the 1940s, why, I churned out novels for publications like *Dime Science Stories* and. . . ."

Jake asked the young woman, "You want me to be on this show of yours?"

"Zap!" said Felony, smiling, hair dancing. "You'll fit right in, Pace! Tonight's topics are Incest, Softball, Tibetan Buddhism and Barrelhouse Piano!"

"Thing is, I'm on a—"

"Be wonderful publicity for your Odd Jobs, Inc. detective agency! Fourteen million people view *Munchin' at Veggies*! And we pipe it into all sixty-three Veggies restaurants in CalSouth! Guarantees you a captive audience of—"

"I'd best not, Miss Fulsom."

"But it'll only take you an hour or so! Little chat with Silly Singleton, play the piano, scoot!"

"You want me to play the piano, too?"

"When I spotted you making your way through this crowd of lit buffs, I said to myself, 'FF, if you can manage to snag Pace to perform his famous Cripple Clarence Lofton medley for the Barrelhouse seg, it'll be a feather in your trap!'"

"Cap," corrected Jake. "Well, I suppose I could maybe fit it in. What time's your show?"

"Be at the Oxnard Veggie's at 6:30 tonight! You'll get away no later than 7:30! Promise!"

"... wrote *Vandals of Vulcan*, my best Captain Cosmos novel, all by my lonesome on a manual typewriter. The letters column in *Heart rending Super Science* was jammed with letters singing its ..."

Nodding, Jake lifted Felony's hand from his arm. "See you at 6:30."

"Zap!" She lunged, hair sizzling, and kissed him on the cheek.

Only about fifty people were interested in hearing Oscar McCracklin lecture on *Robots or Write Groups: Who Produces the Best Fiction?* Fewer than a fourth of the floating plaz seats were occupied.

Jake was near the rear of the small hall, pretending to peruse the tri-op Write Festival program. Actually he ignored the glittering photos of the silver-clad Grubs, hottest novel writing group in the country with three books on the top twenty list, and scanned the others in the room.

A heavyset blond young man two rows up was trying, not quite successfully, to give the impression he wasn't watching Jake. He had on an I——♡ *The Hacks!* tunic and beanie, plus a *Sci Fi Forever!* pennant.

Casually pointing his left hand at the possible plant, Jake punched a tiny button on the detecto belt he was wearing under his shirt.

Brrrtttzzzzz! Whangawhanga! Zzzzzittzzz zrowr!

Damn thing was making those noises again. Jake thought he'd taken care of that when he'd overhauled the belt last month.

Grinning, he gave the belt a furtive whap. Three more got it to cease producing ungodly sounds and noises.

A lean young woman in nudipantz turned around in the seat in front of him and scowled. "We're trying to hear this bald gink, asshole!"

"Forgive me, missy."

"Are you trying to be snide?"

"On the contrary."

"Asshole!" She returned her attention to McCracklin.

He was up on the floating stage explaining how the copperplated writing robot he'd brought with him worked. ". . . 10,000 words a day is nothing for Sluggo here. Not mere words, mind you, but finely crafted prose that . . ."

Jake reached under his shirt, extracted the small scanprint the detecto belt had produced when he'd directed the spynozzle concealed up his sleeve at the suspected opposition agent.

The tiny faxpaper diagram showed that the fellow was carrying a stungun, a kilgun and a two-way combox on his person. Meaning he was more than likely part of the trap that'd been set for Jake.

After crumpling the bit of paper and dropping it in his pocket, Jake pointed his hand at the lecturing McCracklin.

". . . have merely to request that Sluggo turn out prose and he does," the Kirktronics scientist was saying. "Sluggo, what say we write a yarn for the folks to show them how it's done?"

"Okay by me, boss. What genre?"

"Robot's choice."

"Well, I'm sort of in the mood for a mystery . . . Ark! Ark! . . . gather all the suspects . . . you are murderer . . . I was sitting in my office nibbling a rye when she walked in . . . not getting me alive, coppers . . . Ark!"

"Sluggo? What's wrong?"

Jake had pushed a detecto belt button again and that, apparently, had caused the robot to glitch.

Poking his tongue into his cheek, eyeing the ceiling and assuming an innocent demeanor, Jake reached under his clothes and extracted the latest belt printout.

This one showed that McCracklin was wearing a kilgun and that a parasite mindbug was planted behind his left ear. Signals were being broadcast to that control device right now.

Jake pushed another of the buttons on his belt.

Rrrritttzzzzz! Barrangawanga! Zzzzuggggg!

"Is that you again, asshole?"

"Every time I lunch at Veggie's my stomach makes the oddest noises." Standing up, Jake made his way to the exit.

Out in the crowded corridor he took a look at the latest printout. This one told him that whoever was controlling McCracklin was doing it from a room a level below this one.

He decided to go down there.

"You have to get in line, nurfhead!"

"Quit shoving!"

The corridor was thick with lit fans, formed into a rough two column line. Down at the far end two golden-haired young men in one-piece seagreen banglesuits were seated at a small floating plaz table.

"Not trying," explained Jake to the angry fans in his vicinity, "to get into the line, folks. I'm with Drome Security and we have a small little problem along here in Room 26 C."

"Horsepuckey! You're anxious to get autographs from Zip and Digit."

"Quit pushing!"

"Zip and Digit?"

A husky young lady in a *I Lust After the Plagiarists* slinkdress told him, "Up there at the table, boofer. It's Zip . . . isn't he gorgeous looking? . . .the Lead Plotter with the Plagiarists. And . . . isn't he incredibly zappy? . . .Digit, the Backup Copy Editor."

"Oh." Jake resumed cutting through the crowd over to the door he was seeking.

There didn't seem to be any way to sneak up on whoever was controlling McCracklin from down here. Jake decided, therefore, to barge in and take his chances.

"Aren't you Dork?" a lean Chinese girl in a seethru kimonosuit asked him as he elbowed nearer his goal.

"Nope," he assured her, reaching the 26 C door.

"You're not the Dialoguer with the Subliterates?"

"Lady, I just only work for Drome Sec." Smiling amiably at her, he utilized his all-purpose lokpik on the door's system.

Whirring, the door slid open.

Jake crossed the threshold.

 **13**

"That was very impressive," observed Sheldon Sickmann as he shrugged free of his straps and hopped off the cot. "I do wish, though, that he hadn't spilled the soup when you decked him, Mrs. Pace."

"Get over to the door and listen." Hildy was kneeling beside the stretched out servo she'd just disabled. Deftly, she was removing its right arm.

"Been nice if they'd left us our shoes." He tiptoed around the pool of Scotch broth that was growing beside the fallen mech. "Boy, that stuff sure has a pungent odor, doesn't it?"

"Ah." Hildy straightened up, the detached

arm held in her hand like a club. "Any idea what's out in the hall, also who?"

"As I may've mentioned, Mrs. Pace, I awakened in this very room after my stunning and, therefore, haven't seen much else of the surroundings," answered Sickmann, nodding at the neowood door. "This only opened thrice each day, when that robot brought in the meals. Have you ever had cold gazpacho for breakfast?"

"Gazpacho's always served cold." She barefooted over to join him near the doorway.

"I wasn't complaining so much about the soup's temperature as I was about its inappropriateness for the meal that commences the day," Sickmann said. "By the way, how'd you manage to fell our servobot so swiftly and surely?"

"All National Robot & Android mechs have a concealed shutoff presspot in the left armpit. For emergencies."

"Is that so? We pitched the NRA account once, yet I didn't know—"

"Hush for a moment," suggested Hildy.

"Didn't mean to babble. It's simply that, not having anyone to talk to for so . . . Well, I'll be silent while you case the situation."

Hildy pulled the door open inward.

Facing her out in the yellow corridor was a white-uniformed guard. A large freckled fellow who gulped twice at the sudden sight of her before reaching for the stungun in his belt holster.

That small hesitation gave Hildy the advantage.

She swung the borrowed metal arm, bopped the surprised guard on the skull with the fist and soup ladle end.

"Umph," he managed to say.

She whacked him twice more. Caught him as he toppled, dragged him into their room.

Before she discarded the unconscious man on the soupy floor she had his stungun in her left hand. "Let's try to move on out of here, Sheldon," she said quietly.

Sickmann said, "You did a marvelous job of rendering him unconscious."

"I did," she agreed, edging into the hallway.

At twilight Hildy, alone, was flying low over the Bronx Ruins in a skyvan shaped like an enormous cockroach. Below her in the darkening rubble and debris cook fires under cannibal pots were being lit.

When she reached the sector she wanted, a small silver gadget attached to the dash chirped, "Bingo!"

Setting the controls on hover, Hildy unbuckled her safetybelts. After giving her short-cropped chestnut wig a pat and inspecting again the new authentic-looking tattoos on her bare arms, she left the pilot seat.

Through the one-way glaz panel in the belly of the flying cockroach she could see torches bobbing amid the tumbles of old brick and wood. A dozen young men in straw hats and candy-striped blazers were leaping and howling down in the ruins, watching her hovering van.

Reaching back, Hildy flipped on a toktoggle on the control panel. "Hey, Miss Brodsky!"

After a few seconds a lovely voice responded out of a speakgrid. "That damn well better be someone from Roach Reproach, Ltd. up there!"

"Who the frap else'd come out here after dark, sis? It's going to cost you a blinking bundle for this—"

"Oh, don't be ludicrous. It isn't dangerous hereabouts at all," said the voice of Amazon Brodsky. "This is a Double Secure Area and all the Downlevel Townhouses are absolutely safe. Don't let what you see above ground intimidate you. Now, please, get down here and rid me of these unsightly bugs that—"

"Listen, there's a bunch of mean-looking bastards in funny hats down there, lady. I got the feeling they don't mean me any good or—"

"That's only the Minstrels."

"Who are?"

"A new ruins gang. They aren't even cannibals if that's what you're fretting over," said the impatient Amazon. "Anyhow, they can't possibly get through the force dome over my entry hole. And you have an electropass that'll allow you to drop right down from your skyvan. You do have it, don't you? Don't tell me Roach Reproach, Ltd. fouled up on—"

"I got it, I got it, sis, keep your undies on. Thing is, I got to leave my ship hovering up here. I don't want these ginks shooting holes in—"

"They won't," Amazon assured her. "Now hurry on down. I've had a plague of cockroaches down here all afternoon."

"I know, lady, I know." It had cost Hildy fifteen hundred dollars to arrange that.

 **14**

"At long last," sighed Jake, grinning. "I was commencing to think something'd happened to you."

"Several things did," said Hildy.

Jake was in the cabin of his skycar, which was parked on a public landing lot across the street from the Oxnard Veggie's restaurant. On the dash pixphone screen was an image of Hildy, herself again.

"You appear to be in tip-top shape," he said. "But is that a bruise on your arm?"

"A tattoo that won't quite wash off." She rubbed at the dark coiled serpent just above her shapely elbow. "Jake, let me get to the negative stuff right off. They know we're on this case."

"I've arrived at a similar conclusion."

"A two-bit informer named Whispering Wolfbanger saw through my Baroness Eed get up and that—"

"I keep telling you to pay more attention to the tips on disguise I give you when—"

"At any rate, Wolfbanger tipped Amazon Brodsky. Thus, when I hit the *Wretched Mess* set, even though my new guise was foolproof, they were waiting for me."

Jake frowned. "What happened?"

"A couple of louts stungunned me. I awakened a few hours later in a Bowery hospital wing, upstairs from a fragrant soup kitchen. Strapped down."

"They hurt you?"

"Never had the chance. I wriggled free of the straps—"

"You're good at that."

"Yes. Then I got the heck out of there, along with a gent named Sheldon Sickmann."

"Any relation to Krankheit, Sygdom, Machalah, Ugonjwa and Sickmann?"

"He's Sickmann," answered Hildy. "Jake, I think I know what's behind some of this. It involves Wallace Wind, who's—"

"Who's going to have a mindspot session in

a week or so. At which time they'll take him over and control Total Enterprises.''

Hildy said, "Do you also know about Kure?"

"Nope."

"Okay, Kure is something that one of Wind's subcompanies came up with. Sickmann swears the stuff can cure every illness in the book and then some," his wife told him. "Wind wants the agency to test market it, do a whole campaign. Our Brainz, Inc. chums, however, entertain other notions. According to Amazon, they think Kure ought to be withheld and sold only to select customers. Rich select customers who can afford high fees."

"Well, that's sound business theory. You finally got to Amazon Brodsky then?"

"Posing as an exterminator." Hildy rubbed again at the fake tattoo. "I used truth mist on her, shot from a buggun."

"Have they got her mind-controlled?"

"No, she knows what she's doing. When she came in for her prelim tests at Brainz, Inc., they determined she had the sort of larcenous bent that'd make her a good member of the team. The rest of the names on the list Sylvie Kirkyard gave us, though, are under their control."

"Who does Amazon report to, who's her boss?"

"Kevin Kirkyard, poor Sylvie's younger brother." Hildy gave a small, sad shake of her head. "Even her brother was in on the murder plan."

"Yep, I just found much the same thing myself."

"How?"

"I questioned a couple of lads," replied Jake, glancing out the one-way windshield of his skycar. The Veggie's sign, with its chorus of dancing produce, was flashing multicolored across the way. "The fellow who was going to use Oscar McCracklin to lure me into a holding pen someplace, plus a chubby one who they had tailing me. I overcame both of them on a lower level of the Oxnard Sports & Literature Drome. Used truth bugs on 'em both."

"They were working for Kevin Kirkyard?"

"Kevin is in cahoots with Dr. Death and Dr. Sanhamel."

"How about Sylvie's other brother?"

"Ross seems, thus far anyway, clean and innocent."

Hildy touched at her auburn hair. "May I ask, without giving offense, how they knew you were coming and therefore planned a trap?"

"Higby."

"Gee, her gentleman friend is in it, too? Poor kid."

"Nope, no. But he trailed me and—"

"How come?"

"How come what?"

"Higby was trailing you."

"Well, he was lurking in the woods in the corridor of her old digs and he just followed me after I dropped in."

"Saw through your disguise, did he?"

"I wasn't exactly disguised, since this was a simple—"

"Now I don't feel so bad about Whispering Wolfbanger. Go on, dear."

"Kevin and the docs have got Higby's communications system tapped. Soon as he pixed a friend of his to tell him about me . . . Voilà."

Hildy said, "Do you have enough evidence yet to go to the law and get them nabbed for Sylvie's murder?"

Shaking his head, he answered, "Not yet, nope. We also don't have enough to warn Wallace Wind."

"If we tell him what we suspect, he'll—"

"Not Wind. We have to show him vidtapes, printouts, tangible proof or otherwise—"

"But you can't let them get their mitts on—"

"Later this evening, with a possible assist from Steranko the Siphoner, I'm going to see what can be done about tapping Kevin Kirkyard's whole and entire communications system. Likewise those of the doctors Death and Sanhamel."

"Want me to come out there to help out?"

Jake rubbed at his chin. "What happened to Sickmann?"

"He's lying low in the New Haven Redoubt, afraid somebody'll try to snatch him yet again," his wife said. "They obviously don't want him spreading the word about Kure before they get control of Wind."

"You and he part chums?"

"He bestowed his eternal gratitude on me for pulling his chestnuts from the fire. Why?"

"Could he get you into the company that's cooked up Kure?"

"Bedlam Brothers, headquartered in Florida. I don't see why not," she said. "You think we ought to swipe a copy of the formula?"

"Might as well add as many aces to our hand as we can."

"Okay," said Hildy with an affirmative nod. "Oh, one other thing before I sign off. Why aren't you going after Kevin right now?"

Jake looked away from the screen. "Oh, I have a small task to take care of first. Nothing much. So, glad you're safe and—"

"Jake?"

"Hum?"

"What are you contemplating?"

"Nothing."

"Jake."

"Well. it's only a little publicity thing. I'll be

talking about us, plugging Odd Jobs, Inc. and playing the—"

"Is that wise?"

"Kevin and company already know I'm here. Publicity, remember, brings in new cases and income."

"Did you say you'd be playing something?"

"Piano. Playing the piano for a few minutes. My Cripple Clarence Lofton medley on this tradvid show that—"

"Who'd want to hear that?"

"It ties in with one of the featured topics of the evening. Barrelhouse piano and—"

"What show is this exactly?"

"Called *Munchin' at Veggie's.* Reaches millions of homes and there are a lot of wealthy potential clients in CalSouth, Hildy."

"Doesn't it strike you as a mite odd that a television show would include a segment on something as arcane as barrelhouse piano playing? I mean—"

"You forget I was invited to play this very same medley at the International Barrelhouse Buffs Con in Madrid only two years ago."

"Yes, and all of seventy-six people attended, from all over the whole round world. Jake, I really think you better—"

"I'll phone you soon as I'm through, in about an hour. Bye for now, love."

"Jake, you—"

He broke the connection, eased free of the cabin and went jogging across the landing lot toward Veggie's.

Felony Fulsom caught him by the arm when he was but three steps across the mosaic foyer of the vegetarian restaurant. "Tell me something, Pace!" she requested, silver hair crackling. "Are you a good sport?"

"Depends," he replied. "What sort of indignities do you have in—"

"See, Silly Singleton is ill tonight! It's really embarrassing to him! Because what he's got is the Gay Flu and you know the only way you're supposed to get that! But poor Silly's straight as a tie and—"

"Die," corrected Jake. "Straight as a die."

"I'm glad you agree! Anyhow, Pace, Silly's sick and can't handle the telecast tonight! On top of which, his wife's threatening to leave him because she's convinced he must—"

"Who's filling in for him?" Jake scanned the restaurant, which had quite a few potted plants cluttering the main dining room. More plants, in fact, than patrons. Two-thirds of the lettuce-green floating booths were empty.

"Do you like the circus? Well, heck, everybody does! Do you?"

"More or less. Who—"

"Perhaps, being based in the East, you aren't

familiar with our local traditions! But . . . you really wouldn't mind being interviewed by a clown, would you?"

"A clown?"

Felony, electric hair flickering, pointed at a dais all the way across the restaurant. There were four chairs placed there and in one of them slouched a fat man whose face was painted white and green. His nose was a replica of a ripe red tomato, his wig carrot-colored. Flashing neon vegetable silhouettes decorated his yellow suit. "That's Reggie MacVeggie, who's in all our commercials and adored by young and old alike!"

"He has an impressive schnoz."

"Don't let his outward persona lead you astray! He's got an MA degree from Laguna Freeform College!"

"And he's going to do the show tonight, Reggie is?"

"That won't make you too mad and uneasy?"

"Guess not."

She laughed nervously. "You're taking this much better than H. Harry Bangs!"

"How'd he react?"

"He's locked himself in the walk-in vegetable crisper in the galley! It's playing fob with the cooks!"

"Hob."

"Now can you give me the titles of the numbers you'll be doing for your lovely piano medley, Pace?"

From a side pocket he extracted a list. "I wrote them down."

Felony's hair stood straight up, crackling, while she skimmed the faxpaper list. "These sound zappy! 'Strut That Thing,' 'Monkey Man Blues,' 'You Done Tore Your Playhouse Down,' 'Streamline Train,' and 'Juice Joint'! Um ... could we maybe, because of our large and devoted kid audience, clean up the grammar on some of these? For instance, wouldn't 'You Have Torn Your'—"

"Nope."

She gave a resigned shrug. "Well, Pace, I don't want to annoy you too much! You've been a plum about the fact that Silly's—"

"Peach. I've been a peach."

"I don't much like plums either! Now then, I hope you won't scream, stamp your feet, bellow, or anything like that when I tell you what I have to tell you about the piano!"

Jake's left eye narrowed. "What's wrong with the piano?"

"Nothing! Well, except it isn't a piano!" She gestured toward the stage again. "See, they're wheeling it in now!"

"A calliope? You people expect me to play barrelhouse piano on a steam calliope?"

"The piano was broken this morning at a

Brazil War Vets reunion! You can play this thing, though, can't you, Pace?"

The calliope was enormous. All three of the worksuited crewmen were struggling and grunting in getting it upon the stage. The thing was white and gold and formidable.

Jake scratched at the hair over his right ear. "I'll have to try it out first, before the show goes on."

The aroma of the soup of the evening was growing stronger all around. Bulgarian cucumber soup it was.

"That's the attitude I like! Give it a try, come what may!" Tugging on the arm she was grasping, Felony led him through the potted plants and the scatter of diners to the stage. "Reggie! This is Jake Pace!"

"Honk! Honk!" croaked the clown, jumping up and holding out a white-gloved hand.

"Is this a sample of his intellectual approach?" asked Jake while climbing onto the stage.

"He's clowning with you!" explained Felony, remaining on the floor. "Be a mite more intellectual, huh, Reggie!"

"Honk! Honk! Shakespeare!" He executed a wobbly backflip, whapping his bewigged head on the edge of one of the chairs.

"Are you on the sauce again?" She was glaring up at the wobbly clown, hands on hips. "That's all I need! Silly felled with Gay Flu!

That old sci fi coot locked in with the turnips! You high as a bat!"

"Kite," corrected Jake, seating himself at the calliope. He adjusted the gilded stool and studied the keyboard.

"Can you play it?" called Felony, her electric hair fluttering anxiously.

"We'll know soon." He turned the instrument on, rubbed his hands together. "I'll try a simple walking bass to begin."

A few seconds after he touched the keys a bluish mist began hissing up at him from the keyboard.

"Damn, a trap. Hildy was . . ." That was all Jake was able to say before the gas engulfed him and he fell off the stool and into unconsciousness.

 **15**

The view window of Hildy's hotel suite inquired, "Might one change the vista for you, Mrs. Petaluma?"

"No, thanks." She left the glaz slingchair again, walked toward the pixphone alcove.

"We have over sixty delightful views to select from. Perhaps, instead of the lights and towers of the contemporary Manhattan skyline you'd prefer to look back into the past? We can offer you, for example, New York in the romantic 1980s, NYC in the grip of the Great Depression of the 1930s ... That comes with apple vendors, a realistic bread line and—"

"Cease," she advised the voxbox beneath the high, wide window.

"Then perhaps the Sahara at dawn? Moon-light in Vermont? Paris in the ... Woops! Woops!"

Hildy had drawn a small disabler pistol from her thigh holster, used it to stun the talkative mechanism into silence.

"Oy, am I jumpy tonight," she murmured, continuing on her way to the phone.

It was six minutes past midnight, meaning it was six after nine out where Jake was. He was supposed to have contacted her an hour and a half ago.

But he hadn't.

She sat in the tin chair facing the screen and punched out the number of his skycar phone.

No answer this time either.

She tried his hotel.

No answer.

"That damn idiot." Hildy stood, returned to the window and looked at the night outside. "He hasn't that many flaws, but vanity about his piano playing is sure one. Offer him a chance to show off his version of 'You Done Tore Your Playhouse Down' and he'll walk into a nest of vipers or—"

The phone buzzed.

Hildy went sprinting to the alcove. "About time you ... oh."

"The human skeleton I presume," said Ster-anko the Siphoner. "How's tricks, Mrs. P.?"

"What do you want?"

"Have you heard from your long-suffering spouse this evening?"

"Not for several hours. Jake was supposed to phone a couple hours ago, but he hasn't. Do you have any idea what's—"

"I am communicating with you, dear lady, because I am likewise concerned about Jake," said the bald siphoner. "He was due to get in touch hours since."

"Vanity," she said.

"Eh?"

"I think maybe they've conned him into a trap."

"This would be the insidious Dr. Death and crew?"

"Them, yes," replied Hildy. "When Jake called before he was about to go into a place called Veggie's in Oxnard to be interviewed for—"

"Interviewed in Oxnard?"

"They told him they'd let him play the piano on television," she explained. "You know how he is about doing that."

"So you figure they lured him into this vegetable paradise and dropped a net over him, eh?"

"I'm commencing to think so. I just hope they want him out of the way for only a while."

"As opposed to permanently, in the ashes in an urn mode?"

"Could be he's just delayed somehow," admitted Hildy. "But can you find out, from your base there in New Orleans, anything about what might've gone on in that Veggie's restaurant in—"

"Listen, Princess Beanpole, that's my specialty of the house. Gathering info at a distance."

"Okay, do that and also—"

"Listen in on Kevin Kirkyard, Dr. Death, and the Sanhamel broad. I've been doing that for the past hour already. Thus far nothing but nada has turned up," he told her. "You intend to head out West if you don't hear from Jake soon?"

"I'll give him another few hours and then I will, yes," answered Hildy. "Meantime I have an errand to run down in Florida."

"Be of good cheer, Slim," said the siphoner. "I got a hunch our boy ain't defunct yet."

Nodding, Hildy hung up. Then she made one more call, to John J. Pilgrim this time.

Two huge bearded figures loomed up in the rosy Florida dawn. Each was fifty feet high, grinning through its whiskers.

"That's Ches on the right, Wal on the left," said Shelton Sickmann. "No, I take that back, Mrs. Pace. Wal on the right, Ches left."

Hildy glanced at the immense plaz figures that towered on each side of the entrance to the

Visitors' Landing Area of the Bedlam Brothers plant complex as she guided the skycar down through the brightening day. "Impressive," she remarked. "I'd love to have a set for bookends."

After running his tongue over his upper lip, the advertising executive said, "I certainly hope I'm doing the proper thing."

When Hildy nodded her head, the many curls of her raven-tressed wig jiggled, uncoiled and coiled again. The spangles of her short-skirted glittersuit tinkled and flashed. "We need an edge," she said. "And the Kure formula'll—"

"Watch out," he warned, turning away from her, "you've nearly jiggled your ... um ... bosom free of your frock, Mrs. Pace." He coughed into his hand. "I trust you aren't chagrined at having to wear such skimpy apparel."

"I'm not, no." Hildy concentrated on setting the craft down on a pink landing slot. "Now, let's get inside this joint."

"You're confident, are you, that once I sneak you inside the R & D Lab, you can crack the safe they keep the Kure secrets in?"

"I am."

"More Houdini tricks?"

"Raffles," she answered, unbuckling her safety gear and moving, long bare legs flashing in the awakening day, out of the cabin.

"Lordy mama, my ticker!" exclaimed a wheezy voice nearby.

"Morning, Sleepy John," called Sickmann as he joined Hildy.

From out of a small plaz guardhut a thin man in a two-piece unisuit came tottering. Knobby right hand resting on his holstered stungun, he approached them. "Wowie, Mr. Sickmann, that surely is some good-looking heifer you got with you."

"This is Hil ... um ... this is Modest McFadden," introduced the nervous Sickmann, eyes on the pinkish walkway underfoot. "The noted model. Modest, this is Sleepy John Westover, Associate Chief of the Security Police here at Bedlam Brothers."

"Dang if she ain't." Westover patted the vicinity of his heart. "Why, I got that poster of her, one wherein she ain't wearing no more than a wet bowtie, up in my snuggery to home. Mrs. Westover truly loathes and despises that particular work of art. Pleased to meet you, miss."

"Call me Modest," invited Hildy in a silky voice. "And I'll call you Sleepy. Okay?"

"Excuse me a second." He jabbed a hand hurriedly into his trouser pocket, yanked out an atomizer and squirted a yellowish mist in his open mouth. "Calming spray. Keeps me from getting too het up and all."

"How flattering." Hildy leaned close to the guard to smile at him.

"I got to watch my health, you see," explained Westover. "Funny thing is, until I started working here six years back, why, I never worried much about the state of my health at all." He pointed with a knobby forefinger at the complex of Bedlam Brothers buildings. "Being around all this medicine gets you to thinking, though. Just this morning, ensonced here in my hut and perusing a list of symptoms on my computer terminal screen, I pretty near convinced myself I'm coming down with Malzberg's Syndrome."

"Tush." Hildy moved even closer to him. "You're far from lugubrious, Sleepy."

"Wowie dang." He gave himself another whiff of tranquilizing mist.

"Sleepy John, Miss McFadden's going to be doing some tri-op trade ads for Bedlam Brothers Koffstopper Drops," said Sickmann rapidly, after Hildy'd nudged him in the side. "I want to take her inside and show her the lozenge vats."

"Sort of early in the day, ain't it?"

"I have to rush back to Manhattan ever so soon," said Hildy. "I'm due at a nude modeling session for the National Bondage Federation calendar. And you know how long it takes to get all those chains and black leather belts and—"

"Lordy lord, don't tell me no more details,"

pleaded the guard. He took another squirt of mist, then shook some purplish capsules out of a vial and swallowed three or four of those. "I best just buzz you on inside, while I still got a vestige of my health."

"Thank you so much," said Hildy.

 **16**

The four-poster bed creaked and whined as Jake sat up on it.

"I hope you feel better than you look, amigo," said a high-pitched squawky voice. "Because you're about as personable at the moment as the doormat out in front of the Black Hole of Calcutta."

Jake gave his head a few tentative shakes. "Are you a symptom?"

"Absolutely real, señor. Name of Guru," replied the large green and gold parrot perched on one of the ornately carved posts at the foot of the bed. "I always thought you could trust the information in a secret police dossier, but you look a lot older than your thirties to these peepers, chum.''

"Walking into traps, playing calliopes, having knockout gas used on me, exhibiting impressive stupidity—'' Jake told the perched bird—"all take their toll.''

"Your face looks like a prune with a hangover.''

Swinging his legs over the edge of the bed, Jake glanced around. He was in the center of a large shadowy room, a dark-walled shuttered room with only a bedside oil lamp providing light.

Jake sat there, quietly taking inventory of himself. He didn't notice any major aches or pains. There was, however, a sore spot at his right temple.

While he was gingerly inspecting it with a fingertip, the parrot said, "Truthbug.''

"I talked, huh?''

"Like a politician at a picnic, amigo. Even recited some of Ezra Pound's lesser-known cantos before they got you turned off and—''

The sound of sudden kilgun fire, screaming and shouting came rushing in from outside the shuttered windows.

"What's that?''

"Executions,'' answered the parrot, preening his feathers slightly. "These kids always make too much noise.''

"Kids are being killed?''

"No, no, chum. Kids are doing the killing," replied Guru. "A unit of the Death Scouts. They insist on doing in their daily quota of antigov suspects against the outside wall of the studio. Ah, youth."

Jake made a try at standing up, and succeeded fairly well. "Death Scouts? Then I must be in Panazuela."

"The garden spot of Central America, sí," confirmed Guru. "Well, garden spot if you think of gardens as being chock full of bananas and left-wing revolutionaries."

Even though his legs were somewhat wobbly under him, Jake succeeded in getting to the nearest window. Through the slats of the shutter he could see a high stucco wall, its pale peach color glowing in the midday sunlight. Palm trees showed above the top of the wall. He could hear the sound of more killing, but couldn't see down into the street beyond the wall. "You mentioned studio. Does that mean I'm in New Hollywood, the vidmovie complex financed by American investors and—"

"It does indeed, Señor Pace."

This was a new voice.

Turning from the window, Jake saw a slim, dark man of thirty standing beside the antique bed. He wore a tailored three-piece militarysuit of tan and crimson, a visored cap to match. He had twin holsters on his neoleather belt, one holding a kilgun, the other a stungun. Swinging in his right hand, tapping against the tops of his glittering black boots, was a stunrod. The parrot was now sitting on the man's left shoulder.

"You my host?" inquired Jake.

"I am Colonel João Vacaverde of the Secret Police of the Panzuelan Military Junta." His heels clicked, his head bowed.

"And one mean hombre," added Guru, lifting a clawed foot to inspect.

"You working for Kevin Kirkyard?"

Reaching up with his left hand, Vacaverde stroked the parrot. "We have been requested to look after you here for a time, señor," he answered. "It is highly possible you'll be visited in a while, at which time your situation may become further clarified."

"It's also possible I'll bitch to the US government and you goons'll have a million or so shaved off your next rural development loan, colonel."

When Vacaverde laughed and shrugged, the parrot flew from his shoulder to land on a prong of the brass hat tree in a far corner.

The colonel said, "This lovely *casa* was built two years ago for the filming of *The Mystery of the Spooky Mansion*, which the Manhattan *News-Times* of your country awarded two and one half stars and dubbed, 'good of its kind,'" said the soldier. "You may—"

"Faint praise," observed Guru. "A llama turd is good of its kind, but it's still a llama turd."

"We don't even have llamas in this country. Now be silent, my feathered amigo."

"Donkey turd then."

"As I was saying, Señor Pace," resumed the slim colonel, "you are free to roam about this handsome old dark house. You will find a functioning, albeit old-fashioned, kitchen and a well-stocked larder on the ground floor. You may even take the air on the splendid gingerbread porch. Should you, however, make any attempt whatsoever to leave the grounds—"

"It's 'Goombye, Pace!' " interpolated Guru. "Six guards out there at all times. And three of them good enough shots to hit you."

"My little bird exaggerates, señor," smiled the colonel. "There are but five guards. All of them crack shots. Adios."

 **17**

"You're looking a shade smug, Skinny. Had some news about our mutual missing friend?"

"No, Steranko, nothing. But I just acquired something I can maybe use to spring him, if need be."

"Such as?"

"A formula. Now, have you found out anything?"

Hildy's skycar was zooming west through the morning. She was alone again, having sent the uneasy Sheldon Sickmann off to a new and safer hiding place.

On the dash phone screen was Steranko and Siphoner, dressed today in a two-piece funsuit the color of pickled beets. "Since I am in a continual and eternal process of finding out things, your query is redundant."

"So tell me something."

"The *Munchin' at Veggie's* show aired last eve without Jake and his magical piano," said the siphoner. "The regular host was also not in evidence. Jake was seen entering the Oxnard branch of this rabbit-food haven at approximately 6:27 in the PM. No one saw him exit."

"He's still there?"

"Patience, Slim. Allow me to continue my narrative," he said. "At eight last night a large crate labeled FROZEN SPINACH QUICHE was picked up by a skytruck outfit, hauled to the freightport at the Anaheim airfield complex. Destination was Central America."

"Could be they had him in that damn crate. Where in Central America?"

"All I know thus far is that the crate was delivered to the Latino Air Express hangars, which indicates a CA destination."

"How long before you can find out the exact spot it was sent to?"

"Matter of a few more hours."

"Okay, you work on that and I'll go out to CalSouth to see if I can pick up any other leads," said Hildy. "Could be, too, that the crate's just a diversion and Jake's someplace else."

Nodding, Steranko said, "You might want to chat with a lady who has the melodious name of Felony Fulsom. She's the bimbo who lured Jake into the fatal interview."

"Is she pretty and young?"

"Both."

"It figures," said Hildy.

The young man with the glaz stomach asked, "Are you with Sludge, ma'am?"

"What's that the acronym for?" said Hildy, adjusting her silver-rimmed decspecs.

"Nothing. I'm alluding to the Greater Los Angeles Sludge and Sewage Authority." He was sitting in a tin rocker at the edge of the rickety yellow pier that led out a few hundred yards across the small mucky marina. "I was hoping against hope they'd at long last sent someone to inspect our piece of ocean."

"Afraid not." She patted at her butch-cut gray wig. "I have business with Miss Fulsom."

The youth left his chair. He was long and lean and you could see his insides at work through the tinted rectangle set in the front of him. "I noticed you glancing at my window," he said to Hildy.

"Hard to miss." Looking beyond the youth, Hildy scanned the row of half dozen houseboats moored along the swayback pier.

"Be honest, do you find it disgusting and revolting?"

"Not especially, no."

"Few do." He shook his head forlornly. "I thought it would be absolutely repellent. My team of high-priced surgeons concurred. But no such luck."

"Why, if I may ask, did you have it done?"

"You don't know me, huh?"

"Nope."

"Few do anymore. I'm Twitch."

"Pleased to meet you. I'm Beatrix Mixx, with Headhunters, Unlimited," said Hildy with a prim and efficient smile. "Can you tell me which houseboat is that of Miss Fulsom?"

"Third one out. I'm with the Seizures."

"Oh, yes. You were a very successful shock-rock group a few months ago. Whatever happened to you?"

"We live on the fourth houseboat now. We're at a low peak of our careers." He dropped back into the chair, but didn't rock. "Haven't had a platinum vidcaz for weeks. No longer in demmand, no longer objects of frenzied adulation. It's unzappy."

"What do you do in the band?"

"I'm the Lead Fit Thrower."

"Of course, I remember you now." Hildy started walking out on the neowood planks. The smell of the stagnant Pacific was strong in the afternoon air.

"Sewage and sludge wasn't bad enough, oh, no," said Twitch. "Two weeks ago they also began pumping the residue from a chain of ninety-six Wun Cloo Quickie Chinese Food outlets into our water. Look down there amidst the sludge and muck, ma'am. Note the hundreds of crumpled fortune cookie messages, the fragments of thousands of broken chopsticks, the thousands of empty plazpackets of duck sauce. Ugh, it's absolutely disgusting."

"Maybe you could use some of that stuff in your act."

"Hum?"

"Take advantage of the repulsive properties of all this garbage."

"Zam, that's not bad!" Twitch's tin chair whanged twice as he jumped up from it. "Sure, sure, we could roll in it, wallow. Throw it at the audience. Gad, they'd love it." He gave her a thankful pat on the backside. "You've saved our show business lives." He went running out onto the pier.

At a more sedate pace, Hildy followed.

"Shut up, you nitwits!" Felony Fulsom, electric hair turned off, wearing a short terrirobe, shut the last window of her floating parlor.

"The Seizures have been as quiet as a groom for days and days and just when you arrive they—"

"I believe they've had a sudden new inspiration, Miss Fulsom." Hildy was sitting on a glaz divan in the middle of the room.

Returning to a rumphug chair facing her, Felony said, "I'm very flattered, Miss Mixx, that your organization is interested in me!"

"Very much so," Hildy assured her.

From outside, on the next houseboat, came cries of, "Aaargh!" and "Yikes!" The splatter of flung garbage could also be heard.

After scowling at the window, the silver-haired young woman once again studied the tri-op bizcard Hildy'd given her. "Headhunters, Unlimited is just about the biggest personnel procurer in the country!"

"In the world."

"And you have a client who wants to woo me away from Veggies'? At a smarter salary?"

"At double your present salary."

"Zap!" Felony sat up straighter in her chair. "You know, I have been feeling of late that I'm hiding my light under a bush at Veggie's."

"Bushel," corrected Hildy. "All too true. We at HU feel the time has most certainly come for you to move on to the next career plateau."

"Is this new job," asked Felony in a subdued voice, "in a similar capacity?"

Hildy reached into her handbag. "You've heard of Señor Legumbre?"

Felony bounced twice on her seat. "The largest, most successful Mex-Veggie chain of restaurants in America! And they want me to—"

"Have you seen their brochure. It explains the impressive Señor Legumbre success tale quite well." Hildy held a small booklet toward the girl. It had a gleaming golden cover. "Just gaze into the cover, Miss Fulsom. That's right ... gaze deeply as I move this from side to side, back and forth ... keep watching it ... exactly ... back and forth ... making you so sleepy ... so very sleepy ... That's right ... lean back in your chair ... Now we'll have a chat."

"A chat," echoed the hypnotized young woman.

"Where's Jake Pace?"

"I don't know."

"You lured him into the Oxnard Veggies' last night."

"I was hired for that."

"By whom?"

"Dr. Sanhamel. A job with Brainz, Inc. would also pay better than Veggies' and—"

"What happened to Jake?"

"They used knockout gas on him."

"Administered how?"

"Through the calliope."

"Calliope?"

"When he sat down to rehearse his nitwit barrelhouse tunes."

"Vanity," said Hildy. "Okay, he was knocked cold. Then what?"

"Reggie MacVeggie and I had to pretend he'd been taken suddenly ill. He hauled him off the stage and into the kitchen. We were supposed to stash him in the vegetable walk-in crisper, except that old poop H. Harry Bangs was still hiding in that. We put him in the root cellar instead. Until they came for him."

"Who came?"

"Dr. Sanhamel and a couple of other fellows. All decked out as skytruckers. Not hard for her to look like one, with her build."

"What'd they do with him?"

"Nailed him up in a crate, put him in their skytruck, flew off."

Hildy hesitated, then asked, "He was still alive?"

"Sure. They don't want to kill him, I don't think."

Hildy smiled at that. "You don't have any idea where Dr. Sanhamel was taking him?"

"No, none."

"Did she mention Central America?"

"No."

Hildy put her hands on her pretty knees. "Well, sir, I guess I'm going to have to look up Dr. Rose Sanhamel."

"Let me save you the trouble, dear," offered a gruff voice behind her.

 **18**

Jake was seated in the huge hollow dining room of his haunted house prison, just about to start in on the dinner he'd prepared himself, when Kevin Kirkyard came strolling in. "Ah, mine host," said Jake, grinning thinly.

"Holy cow," observed Kevin, his plump boyish face registering puzzlement. "You sure are an odd one, Pace. Fixing yourself a spinach quiche for dinner, after we hauled you down here in a frozen spinach quiche crate."

"So that's what gave me the notion?" He set aside his plastic knife and fork.

"That's right, you were dead to the world the whole darn trip. Must be subliminal." He took a chair down from the head of the table where

Jake was. "Listen here, Pace, I've got to admit you're giving us a slight pain in the butt."

"How so?"

"Gosh, go ahead and chow down. I don't want to screw up your meal." Kevin rested his elbows on the tabletop, waited for Jake to pick up his knife and fork again. "Darn sorry about the cheesey silver. But, you know, we decided plastic was a heck of a lot safer."

Jake began eating, saying nothing.

"Where was I? Oh, yeah, you're futzing things up for us, you know, Pace," said Sylvie's younger brother. "C'mon, where's my sister?"

"Scattered over the Pacific Ocean."

"Not that one. I mean the simulacrum that jerk McCracklin built on the sly."

"A sim?" Jake chewed a bite of quiche. "You Kirktronics folks can do just about anything. My my."

"Leapin hyenas, Pace!" said Kevin, growing annoyed. "Will you, you know, quit horsing around. We already used a truthbug on you."

Jake rubbed at his temple. "Then you know where the andy is."

"It's not there anymore."

"Oh, so?"

"I sent a crew to Iola, Wisconsin to pick up the darn thing," explained the young man. "Wasn't there."

"Well, that's certainly news to me."

144

Kevin said, "When we pumped you, there were some blocks. Mental gates, you know, that you've learned to apply so that when you're quizzed by your opponents you don't spill your guts right off." He chuckled. "But we got around those. Heck, Kirktronics makes the best truthbug on the market."

"Then you must know just about everything I do," Jake told him. "By the way, when you were in there, did you find out anything about where I may've left my plaid skycar cap? Misplaced the darn thing about three weeks back and, for the life of me, Kev, I can't remember where—"

"Holy H. Crow! Talk about gall," exclaimed the angry Kevin. "Here you're our prisoner and yet you go wising off like—"

"Gallows humor," explained Jake. "If the android replica of your late sister isn't in Wisconsin, I don't know where the hell it is." Obviously Hildy, who must know he'd been grabbed, had arranged to move their client to a new hideaway.

Kevin eyed him. "No kidding?"

"Cross my heart."

"Heck." Kevin dropped his elbows off the table, let his hands rest in his lap. "Then your wife must be the one who sent that bleeding heart shyster to take her."

"Who'd that be?" asked Jake as he finished his wedge of quiche.

"John J. Pilgrim."

Jake merely nodded.

Kevin's elbows returned to the mahogany tabletop. "We can't find a trace of Pilgrim," he confided. "Where is he?"

"I'd wager (A) a saloon, (B) a bar, (C) a cocktail lounge, (D) a liquor store or (E) a winery."

"We know the guy bends the elbow," said Sylvie's brother. "What I want to know from you, Pace, is where the dickens did he take my Sis?"

Jake grinned. "That's a nice touch of sentiment, calling her Sis," he said. "Did you refer to her as Sis while you sat around and planned how to kill her?"

Sitting up straight, Kevin said, "I didn't want her to die, you know. But I was outvoted. Dr. Death said it'd be better all around to get rid of her for good and the others agreed."

"One of the perils of democracy, the majority rule. Here in idyllic, tropical Panazuela your pal Generalissimo Brazo Obrigado runs things much more efficiently."

"Holy cow, that greaseball's no friend of mine," protested Kevin. "We've got him mind-controlled, which is how come we can use New Hollywood as a base and all."

Jake poured himself a glass of white grape juice. "And Wallace Wind is the next one you take over, huh?"

"Darn right," answered Kevin with a chuckle. "Once he's ours, boy, we'll really go places." He chuckled a bit more. "And once that happens, of course, we'll let you go, too."

"I somehow doubt you."

"No, no bull, Pace. Once we've got old WW in our pocket, why, heck, we'll control 56 percent of everything," he said. "Do you have any idea what the net income on 56 percent of everything is?"

"A tidy sum."

"Darn right," agreed Kevin. "So, just as soon as we control Wind, you'll be turned loose. We'll, you know, have to diddle with your brain a little. That's so you won't remember anything about us, what we're up to and all. A simple mindwipe'll take care of that, Pace. We won't need lazsurgery or anything grim."

"Suppose you don't find the replica of your murdered sister?"

"We have to find her, because she knows nearly as much as you," he said. "And we'll find her, don't worry. If you don't know where Sis is, then your wife must. We'll get her to—"

"If you bastards try—"

"Easy, Pace, stay put." He suggested with a downward wave of his hand that Jake sit again.

"You try to touch me and that guard in the hall'll use a stungun on you. Why spend most of your stay in Panazuela flat on your butt unconscious?"

"Why indeed?" Jake sat again.

19

Dr. Rose Sanhamel was thickset, broad-shouldered. Her graying brown hair was close-cropped and she wore a two-piece blue bizsuit. In her right hand was a stungun, pointed at Hildy. "You brought off the hypnotizing of little Felony here quite well, darling," she complimented. "Of coure, her teenie weenie brain isn't all that difficult to control."

Slowly Hildy turned her chair until she was facing the doctor on the threshold. "You've got this place bugged?"

"Dear, we've got just about everything you can think of bugged and tapped." She took a few heavy steps into the parlor.

"What about my husband?"

"He seems nowhere near as bright as you, Hildy." She shook her head. "Walking right into our clutches like that."

"Jake has a few weak spots," his wife conceded. "Where is he?"

"Exactly where you'll soon be, sweetheart."

"Can you be a bit more specific?" Hildy looked beyond the husky woman. There didn't seem to be anyone out on the houseboat's deck.

"Right now I'm more interested in asking questions rather than answering them."

Casually, Hildy crossed her long legs, letting one booted foot swing slowly back and forth. "He's alive, though?"

"Listen, darling, we make it our policy to kill as few people as possible."

"But you made an exception with Sylvie Kirkyard."

"She was making a real first-rate nuisance of herself," said the doctor. "And since she owned a nice chunk of Kirktronics, it seemed wiser to send her on to glory."

"And she thought of you as one of her few trusted friends."

Dr. Sanhamel laughed. "Sylvie was a sweet thing, but a very lousy judge of character," she said. "Trusting me, hiring you. Not smart."

"I don't completely agree, since Odd Jobs, Inc. has done a pretty fair job of finding out what you buffoons are up to and—"

"Really won't do you a bit of good, dear," the doctor assured her. "A simple mindwipe and you'll recall not a smidgin about Brainz, Inc., poor Sylvie, or anything else that matters. Now then, I'd very much like you to tell me where the sim is."

"Which sim'd that be?"

Coming yet closer, keeping her stungun aimed at Hildy's breast, Dr. Sanhamel said, "We know about McCracklin's getting a dupe of Sylvie's mindspot into an android rep of her body, and we know that she hired Odd Jobs, Inc., darling."

"Then you ought to know where the andy is, too."

"We know where it *was*," said the hefty doctor. "But Sylvie's no longer with your friend Moneyback Smith in Iola, Wisconsin. He tells us that the noted radical attorney, John J. Pilgrim, spirited the sim away just hours before we arrived."

"Fancy that?" Hildy was still swinging her foot back and forth.

"Not that a truthbug stuck to your skull is all that painful," said Dr. Sanhamel. "But it'd be less painful for you if you told me now."

"Yes, I really am not fond of pain very much," admitted Hildy, tangling her fingers in her wig. "I suppose, actually, that's a flaw in my character. I mean, Jake's often pointed out that a first-class private operative ought to be able to stand—"

Wwwwwiiisssssshhh! Kathump!

The toe of her right boot, activated by a special triggering pressure of her big toe, had become a small hard missile that went whizzing free of the boot and right into the approaching Dr. Sanhamel's midsection.

"Oof," commented the doctor as she doubled up.

Hildy was out of her chair, kicking out with her left foot.

Thunnnngggg!

She kicked the stungun free of the doctor's thick fingers, lunged, caught the weapon before it hit the parlor thermorug.

"Dear, you're not behaving in . . . Unk!"

Hildy kicked her again, in the backside this time.

Dr. Sanhamel went stumbling across the floating room until her head bonked into the arm of the chair the hypnotized Felony was still occupying.

Swiftly, Hildy followed the doctor. She delivered three chopping, side-handed blows to her thick neck.

The doctor sighed like a dying set of bagpipes, slumped down into a tired dog position on the parlor floor.

Hildy knelt with one knee in her broad back

as she slapped her own truthbug against the doctor's temple. She said, "Soon as I make sure you don't have any minions on the deck, I'll get back to you. We'll have that conversation you're so anxious about."

The long straight underground corridor smelled of clay and paint. On each side of Hildy were glaz windows giving views of robots at work fashioning jugs and pots out of clay. Farther along she passed the rooms where six armed 'bots painted and decorated the pottery with authentic Indian designs.

Hildy was walking briskly, even though the opaque plyosack slung over her shoulder contained the unconscious form of Dr. Rose Sanhamel.

At the corridor's end she tapped on a turquoise metal door.

Faintly from the other side came the sound of piano thumping and singing.

". . . I ain't the resurrectionist and I ain't the resurrectionist's son . . ."

Hildy tapped again, harder.

"But I can revive your pussycat until the . . . Eh? A knock without."

A moment later the blue door hissed aside to reveal a rumpled John J. Pilgrim swaying in the doorway.

"Everything okay?" asked Hildy, carrying her cargo into the underground room.

"As okay as things can be in a hideaway sixty feet under, of all the ungodly places, Bixby, Arizona," answered the tipsy attorney. "A hideaway in the bowels of the Authentic Amerind Pottery Co."

"Whatever do you have there, Mrs. Pace?" The Sylvie Kirkyard android was sitting on a floating armchair, a faxmagazine open on her lap.

Dumping the heavy sack to the floor, Hildy said, "Don't get upset now, Sylvie. You already know, don't you, that Dr. Sanhamel double-crossed you?"

"Is that she?" Standing, she pointed with her right shoe toe at the lumpy bundle on the neoparquet.

"It is, yes."

Crossing, Sylvie circled the sack. "There's no doubt about her being on the other side?"

"None. She's in with Dr. Death and your brother Kevin. She helped plan your murder."

"Is she dead in there?"

"Merely stunned. Odd Jobs, Inc. rarely kills people."

"Softies," muttered Pilgrim as he went zig-zagging to the small upright green piano against the wall.

"John J," said Hildy, "the doctor'll be unconscious for at least another dozen hours, due to the setting on the stungun I used to pacify her after I finished with my questioning. I want her stored in the room next to this one. Okay?"

"I could have the robots bake and glaze the old dear," offered the lawyer, seating himself at the keyboard.

"No rough stuff, no funny stuff," warned Hildy. "I may have to use her to bargain for Jake."

"Why not do that right now?" asked Pilgrim.

"Because I'm just not sure they'll make a trade."

"I sure as hell would. Give me a fat old bimbo over Jake Pace any day."

"Be that as it may," said Hildy. "This bunch isn't exactly tenderhearted. I've got another notion about how to spring Jake from their clutches. Should that not work, I'll try bargaining with them for the doctor."

"Where is Mr. Pace?" Sylvie returned to her seat. "I hate to think he's in jeopardy because of what he's been doing on my behalf."

"Jake's in trouble mostly because he fancies himself a crackerjack piano player." Hildy glanced over at Pilgrim, who had his stubby fingers poised above the keys. "They're holding him down in Panazuela, in New Hollywood."

"Generalissimo Obrigado is one of the important people they already control," said Sylvie.

"They've had their main Central American headquarters in New Hollywood ever since they took him over.

Pilgrim rested his hands on the keys. "You planning to go down there and risk your pretty neck to save that dimbulb hubby of yours, Hildy?"

Hildy went over to the pixphone table. "I've grown habituated to him."

"There are cures."

"Don't play anything for a while," she warned. "I have to call Steranko the Siphoner."

 **20**

Lounging casually on the midday porch of his Victorian mansion, Jake took in the activities of the New Hollywood movie lot. A few hundred yards away rose a Foreign Legion fort, surrounded by several square yards of burning sand. A half dozen young women in one-piece glittering shortsuits were rehearsing a tap-dance routine in the courtyard of the yellow-brick fortress. A number, Jake had found out from the only one of his guards who'd converse with him, for an upcoming vidmovie entitled *Beau Geste Follies*.

The moderately friendly guard was stationed in Jake's front yard, beside a plaz replica of a bronze elk. Although watching the tapdancers, the heavyset guard was also aware of Jake and turned to eye him every minute or so. He carried a stunrifle, had a kilgun on his belt.

Beyond the fort to the right you could see a stretch of midtown Manhattan as it was supposed to have looked way back in the 1940s. They were taping a scene for *Zombies On Broadway II*. Rising up on the left was the false front of an opera house, being used in the detective thriller *Walter Wang At The Opera*. Farther off was the pleasant Heartland main street where they'd be staging the big dance finale of *Bodysnatchers of 2005*.

Jake had a clipboard on his lap and as he rocked on the porch swing he made an occasional note.

Diversion?

Kitchen?

Too obvious?

Well, obvious or not, diversion might be his best bet. Rig up an explosion in the big gloomy kitchen of the old dark house, using the old-fashioned gas stove and a few simple ingredients from the pantry. An explosion complete with lots of noise and smoke. That would distract the guards.

All of them?

Nope, you couldn't be certain. Maybe only three at best out of his set of five around-the-clock guards would go rushing into the house to see what was going on wrong. Let that problem sit for a bit.

New identity?

Simplest thing would be to use a couple of bedsheets to become an Arab raider. Decked out that way, Jake ought to be able to mingle with the extras who'd be working at the fort this afternoon.

Zombie?

Converting himself into a walking dead man and mingling with the cast of the zombie film had a certain appeal. For one thing, it was a greater challenge to his acting abilities. And to his ingenuity, since he'd have to improvise both costume and makeup from what could be scrounged up inside the mansion.

Vanity!

Probably so. Yep, if Hildy were here she'd remind him that this was not a time for showing off his, admittedly, considerable talent as an actor. What was called for in this situation was a simple dodge. Something quick, easy, and effective. Meaning the desert raider was a better—

"Good morning, Señor. You look less ruined today."

"Morning, Guru. Where's your perch?"

"The esteemed colonel is elsewhere," answered the parrot, settling on the porch rail. "Writing a scenario, are you?"

Jake took up the top sheet of paper, crumpled it and tucked it into his pocket. "Notes for my diary."

"I thought perhaps you'd caught New Hollywood fever, amígo, and were contemplating becoming part of the industry."

"I imagine I could turn out a fair script if I . . ." Jake paused, frowning and then sniffing.

"Something is wrong, Señor?"

Jake looked over at the guard some forty feet off, then back at the bird. "A mech replica has a special scent, especially a new one," he said. "Guru was a real parrot, you ain't."

"Ten bonus points for the famed Pace schnoz," said the parrot. "You're correct, I'm a sim."

"Where's the real thing?"

"In custody." the mechanical replica of Guru took a few steps along the railing, hopped, wings flapping, and landed beside Jake on the swing seat. "I brought a message."

"Which is?"

"Stand by," said the false Guru.

"That's it?"

"What do you expect from a parrot, amígo, a recitation of the collected poems of Rudyard Kipling?"

Jake asked, "How long do I stand by?"

"No longer than nightfall." The parrot left the swing, went flying up into the bright day. "Adiós."

On a fresh sheet of paper Jake wrote one word.

Trap?

He was in the kitchen an hour or so later, squatting to inspect the deep oven of the gas stove, when Kevin Kirkyard came barging into the room.

"Holy cow, am I ticked off at you," Sylvie's brother announced.

Jake rose to face him. "Any special reason?"

"A bunch, buddy, a whole stewpot of reasons." Boyish face flushed, he held up his left hand with the fingers spread wide. "First, the damn parrot."

Moving away from the stove, Jake seated himself at the kitchen table. "Cookie?" he inquired, taking one for himself from the plate.

"No, no, I don't want a goshdarn cookie." He was clutching his little finger with the thumb and forefinger of his other hand. "Seems to me a guy who bakes cookies all the time is a sissy, but I haven't, you know, got the darn time to go into that topic right now. One, the dark parrot."

"You mean Guru?"

"How many other darn parrots are there?"

"Let's see." Jake narrowed his left eye, gazed ceilingward. "The last parrot census in Panazuela was carried out in 1999 and the figures have probably—"

"Guru! I'm talking about Colonel Vacaverde's beloved pet," said Kevin. "He's vanished."

"Birds do that frequently. It's called flying the coop."

"You're the last one who saw him."

"Oh, so?"

"Right out there on your porch it was, Pace. Ramirez saw it."

"That's the name of the guard next to the elk, Ramirez?"

"Yes, yes. Ramirez says you and Guru were extremely chummy."

"I've always had a way with—"

"What the heck did you do, Pace, bribe that halfwit bird to fly over the wall with a message for—"

"How the hell would you go about bribing a parrot?"

"If it can be done, you're the sneaky so and so to do it," said Kevin. "I know the bird's missing and—"

From the afternoon outside came the sounds of further executions by the Death Scouts.

"Kids nowadays," muttered Kevin. "Okay, let's get to item two. Dr. Sanhamel."

"She's missing, too?"

"You know darn well she is."

Jake grinned, took a bite of his coconut cookie. Not enough honey, he decided after a moment.

"Where is she? Where's Dr. Rose?"

"Has it occurred to you," suggested Jake, after another bite of cookie, "that she and Guru may've run off together?"

"Oh, funny, Pace. Just as funny as a . . . as a . . ."

"Grunion?"

Kevin took an angry step back. "Quit needling me about Sylvie!"

"I was just trying to help you finish your simile, Kev."

"Sure, sure. You know Sylvie went up to Oxnard as a kid for the grunion runs. You know we scattered her ashes in the drink off—"

"After faking a note," said Jake. "Ever read up on the effects of Asthmaline? About what it does to its victims. Now, the way you administered it to your sister, the first thing that must've happened was—"

"Just shut up!" warned Kevin. "Dr. Death worked all that business out. And it's painless. It's an absolutely painless way to die."

"Is it?"

"Oh, go to blazes." Spinning on his heel, Kevin left the kitchen and went slamming out of the mansion.

Jake helped himself to another cookie.

21

"I am very much upset about my parrot," said Colonel Vacaverde.

"What man wouldn't be," sympathized Jake. "Guru was one smart bird."

The two of them, followed by four thoroughly armed guards, were walking in the twilight across the New Hollywood lot.

"I am not especially fond of the use of torture," the dapper colonel explained as they moved through a dusty Old West street, "even though I earned excellent grades in the subject while attending the Academy of Counter Revolutionary Tactics up in your country a few years ago, Señor Pace."

Jake avoided a ball of tumbleweed that came drifting along. "I'm glad to hear—"

"However, unless you tell us where my dear little Gurito has flown to, I'll see to it that—"

"That why we're going to the Front Office?"

"Sí, I fear Señor Kirkyard has reached the limit of his patience," said the military man. "After brooding over his unsatisfactory interview with you this afternoon, and consulting with key advisors such as myself, he's decided to use various sophisticated Kirktronics implements of interrogation on you."

"Doesn't sound like it'll be much fun."

"It won't," Vacaverde assured him.

"I've always considered myself," said Kevin as he paced the huge black and white office, "to be one of the good guys."

"That might be self-delusion," suggested Jake from the ebony slingchair he'd been ordered to sit in.

"I mean, heck, I try to be nice to everybody."

"With the possible exception of your late sister."

Kevin gave Colonel Vacaverde, who was standing near the doorway, an exasperated look. "See what I mean about this darn guy all the time mouthing off?"

Nodding, the colonel said, "He is, I'm afraid, incorrigible, Señor Kirkyard. We had better escort him to the Prop Warehouse so—"

"Prop Warehouse?" said Jake.

"Oh, that's where we keep the torture ... um ... the interrogation equipment," Kevin told him. "What say, Pace, are you going to let me keep being a nice person who doesn't use this sort of gadget? Just tell us what your wife and your underlings have done with Dr. Rose Sanhamel."

"Her current whereabouts are unknown to me," said Jake. "Likewise those of the parrot."

"Gosh, do you have any idea how you've futzed things up for us?" Kevin came over to scowl down at him. "Because you people have grabbed Dr. Rose and the poop may hit the fan any time, Dr. Death's had to move everything up. We're going to have a go at Wally Wind tomorrow."

"Tomorrow, huh?"

"Do you have any notion how damn tough it is to reschedule an appointment with a man as powerful as WW? Especially since—"

"Señor Kirkyard," cut in Colonel Vacaverde politely, "might one suggest we get on with the questioning of this man?"

"Yeah, yeah, you're darn right, Colonel." Turning his back, Kevin walked away from Jake. "It's just that he gets me so darn annoyed with his smug—"

"You can't! No, please."

The far door of the Front Office had come

swinging open. A lovely young black woman was coming into the room backwards.

She was trying to block the entry of a small frizzy-haired blond man in a full-length neomink overcoat.

Kevin blinked. "What the heck is—"

"One seems to be havin' a deuced beastly time gettin' in here for a powwow, ducky," drawled the intruder.

"Evelyn? Is that you?" asked Kevin.

"Jolly well better be, old thing, or me old mom was given a fast shuffle at the Liverpool Maternity Ward some years back."

"Evelyn Alabaster," said Kevin, chuckling. "Boy the best darn movie director in England. And you're going to be working for us here in New Hollywood."

"Best bloomin' director in the whole bloody world." The small man edged around the perplexed secretary, bounded over to Kevin, and hugged him. "I'm so bloody eager to get going on our movie that I, don't you know, popped over here two whole bloomin' days early."

"Well, that's terrific, gee." Kevin got himself free of the little director's furry embrace. "The thing is, I'm sort of in the middle of some . . . um . . . Kirktronics business right now."

"Commerce," sneered Alabaster. "I'm talkin' art, ducks. Our little remake of *Little Caesar* is goin' to be a gem of purest . . . Gadzooks!"

He'd just noticed Jake sitting there. "Who's this handsome bloke?"

"Nobody," answered Kevin quickly. "Just a, you know, business associate. Colonel, why don't you escort him over to the Prop Warehouse and I'll join—"

"Just hold your bloomin' horses, old pip," said the director as he waved them back and approached Jake himself. "Can't you see who this is?"

"I *know* who it is, Evelyn," said Kevin a bit impatiently. "Now if you'll allow the colonel to—"

"That face. It's absolutely wizard, don't you know." Alabaster was studying Jake's head through a frame made by his hands. "He's perfect, dead cert perfect, old bean, for the part of Rocco."

"He's not an actor," said Kevin. "He doesn't want to be an actor."

"Let the perishin' bloke speak for himself, Kevin love."

"Well," said Jake, pretending to consider the matter, "I've always felt I'd make an excellent actor. Particularly in a crime drama, which I presume your production is—"

"Blimey! That'll be tophole. That face, that bloomin' face and your voice. You're the perfect doomed gangster, me lad." The diminutive director tugged Jake up out of his chair so that he might administer a bear hug. When his lips were near Jake's ear, he whispered, "How am I doing, Jake?"

"Accent's awful, but otherwise not too bad."

"Wait'll you see act two," said Steranko the Siphoner.

Kevin had succeeded in getting everyone seated around the big office. "Onita," he instructed his secretary, "go out now, shut that door and don't allow anyone else to enter until I give you the—"

"In a porky's valise," said the beautiful green-haired young woman who came barreling into the Front Office. "Nobody's going to keep Tender St. Germain cooling her fanny in the foyer." Her two-piece skintight banglesuit tinkled and glittered as she went striding over to where the disguised Steranko was seated.

"Listen, lovenest," he said, holding both hands up in front of himself for protection, "there was no bloomin' need, really now, for you to come followin' me from Greater Los Angeles."

"Nertz," observed Hildy, tossing her green hair angrily. "You promised me a part in this flick you're lensing with these beaners and then you dump me in—"

"Who the heck is this woman?" Kevin wanted to know.

"I'm Tender St. Germain," said Hildy, turning her attention to him. "Do you mean to sit there on your fanny and tell me you've never ever seen me on the silver screen?"

"Well, actually, I don't see all that many movies. Oh, sure, we make them, but—"

"You mean you never saw me in *Fourteen Sexmad Rapists?*"

"Gosh, no. Now if you'll just—"

"Nor *Eleven Escaped Bloodsuckers?*"

After shaking his head, Kevin pointed at the open doorway. "Miss . . . um . . . St. Germain, we happen to be holding a pretty important meeting just now. So if you wouldn't mind—"

"I suppose the furtherance of my cinema career isn't important? I suppose the fact that this little nurf promised me a lead in—"

"Ducksy, we can work all this out." Steranko, wrapping his fur coat around himself, walked over to the door. "You pop out, get yourself a nice bedsitter at the bloomin' Sheraton-New Hollywood and soon as—"

"Didn't you even catch my perf in *Fifteen Demented Butcher Boys?*" Hildy asked Kevin.

"Evelyn, please, get this lady the heck out of—"

"What you need, honeybun," said Hildy, reaching deep into her bangled shoulder bag, "is a nice copy of my resumé. All in full color, with tri-op shots of me in provocative—"

"Leave it with Onita and I'll look at it, I promise, soon as we . . . Oops!"

Hildy had produced not a resumé but a stungun.

Zzzzzzzummmmmmm!

As Hildy's pistol sent a stunbeam straight at Kevin's chest, Steranko did three things. He closed the door with a bump of his furred backside, yanked out a stungun of his own and shot Colonel Vacaverde before he could jump up and use his stunrod.

"My," said the secretary, looking from Kevin to the colonel as they stiffened and toppled floorward.

Tucking her stungun away, Hildy said to Jake, "Glad to see you."

"Same here." Jake put his arms around his wife and kissed her.

"Hey, folks, cut the mush, huh?" advised the siphoner. "We're got to get our tokes on the road and away from sunny, fun-filled Panazuela."

Jake moved back from Hildy. "You don't look all that bad with green hair."

"Matches my eyes." She pointed a foot at the slumped Kevin. "We have Dr. Sanhamel safely in storage, but I don't think we're going to be able to haul this one out of here."

Jake asked, "How long is he out for?"

"I have my stunner set for twelve hours."

"Better give him a dose that'll last twenty-four," said Jake. "And the secretary also."

"Listen, I assure you," said Onita, "I'm not going to confide in anyone what went on in—"

"Probably not, but we can't risk it."

"Is even twenty-four hours going to be enough time to clean up this whole mess?" asked Steranko.

"Has to be," Jake told him. "They've modified their plans and they're going after Wallace Wind tomorrow."

"Oh," said Hildy.

 **22**

It was snowing in Gnordling, Finland.

Heavy snow, dropping straight down through the midday sky. It hid most of the buildings outside the viewindow of the hotel suite.

Jake was tugging on the top half of a two-piece dark blue blazersuit in front of a wall mirror in the living room area. "If your information's correct, this ought to work out just—"

"After all we've been through, Jacob, how can you doubt that I've yet again come up with the straight scoop." The siphoner, gotten up now in a two-piece tweedsuit, ginger moustache and plaid bowler, was sitting on a neowood bench near the big window. "Trust me, *she's* the reason Wallace Wind is spending today and tomorrow at his estate on the outskirts of Gnordling."

"The G is silent," mentioned Hildy as she came in from the bedchamber area. She had long blonde hair, done up in intricate braids, and wore an embroidered three-piece folksuit.

"I wish you were likewise, Slimjim."

"Your moustache isn't quite right," Hildy told him.

"Sure, it is. Isn't it, Jake?"

He glanced away from the mirror. "Isn't as droopy as that favored by the real Inspector Wayland-Stonebruce of New Scotland Yard."

After tugging at both ends of the fake moustache, Steranko asked, "Better?"

"Passable," said Hildy, crossing over to Jake.

"Damn lucky your pal the inspector is attending the Sixth Annual International Murder Games here in Guh-Nordling as a judge," said Steranko, "and was willing to let me impersonate him for a half day or so."

"Also fortunate he's undersized and puny," said Hildy. "Otherwise you wouldn't be able to approximate him."

"Geeze, Skinny. Here I am, fresh from saving Jake from the clutches of the unrighteous and—"

"What say," Jake suggested to them, "you both call a truce for the duration?"

Steranko gave his moustache another careful tug. "I am merely stating facts about how noble

I've been. There's an old saying about knowing the truth and the truth shall—"

"Okay, I appreciate your helping me rescue Jake."

"Helping? I master-minded the whole and entire—"

"Tell me some more about Wispy O'Ruddy," requested Jake.

"You already know she's here in Guh-Nordling as a member of the American Murder Game Team," said Steranko. "The lass is twenty-two, five foot three, weighs one hundred twenty-six pounds, has—"

"A mite on the chubby side," observed Hildy.

"All bimbos don't model themselves after fence poles, memsahib. To continue. Wispy and Wind have been having an affair, or what passes for an affair when one of the participants is twenty-two and the other eighty-seven. Been going on for lo! these many weeks. Since WW can buy off scandalmongers and gossip columnists, few know of the torrid romance. Your 'umble servant is one of the happy few."

Jake adjusted a short-cropped blond wig on his head. "She'll have access to the Wind chateau in the hills beyond town."

"Exactly."

"Okay. At the moment, Wispy O'Ruddy thinks I'm Boxboy Shuster, a roving correspondent for Int Vidwall, who is anxious to tape an interview with her on the eve of the first round of the Murder Games," said Jake.

Hildy gave his wig a small tug from behind. "There, it's straight now."

Tilting his head to the left, Jake studied his image. "Anything on Dr. Death, Steranko?"

"Oops, all this dressing up distracted me," he said. "According to my sources, Dr. Death is en route to Guh-Nordling for his appointment with the aging tycoon. He's due to arrive at 6:04 PM, Finnish time. He is not in the most cheerful of moods."

"Does he know about what went on at New Hollywood?"

"Yep, Master Kirkyard's stupefied body was discovered early this AM by one of the Colonel Vacaverde's concerned toadies. The news has wended its way to Dr. D."

"He'll be extra cautious, since he's aware how much we know," said Jake.

"From what I hear," said Steranko, "he is always extra cautious."

Jake and his botcamera waited on the snowy stone porch of the American Murder Games Team Pavilion for a full two minutes before the realoaken door was opened.

"Excuse me," said the slim, dark-haired young woman in the doorway. "I was working out."

"Are you up to answering doors?"

"Hum?"

"That knife in your chest." He pointed at the bloody weapon protruding from her bosom.

"I'd have thought that someone who was covering the games for television, and interviewing obvious people like Wispy O'Ruddy, would know we never use *real* weapons." She scanned him thoroughly up and down.

Jake gave her a dazzling smile, flashing his freshly capped teeth. "Hey, just kidding, little lady," he said. "Don't you know about the ol' Boxboy's habit of legpulling?"

"You might as well come in." She drifted away from the threshold. "I'll take you to Wispy."

The shoulder-high robot camera shrugged the snow off its pebbled gray surface and rolled into the pavilion's long, tiled hallway after Jake.

"A bit downcast, aren't you?" Jake said at the young woman's slim back.

"I'm not downcast," she replied. "The reason I'm less than jolly is that the coach shifted my place in the offensive lineup at the last minute."

"Isn't the victim on the defensive team?"

"Of course," she said, tugging the prop knife free of her chest. "This victim stuff is just something I was practicing on myself with. After all, in real play the opposition team picks the victim. Do you really know so little about—"

"Kidding again." He tried another personable smile on her.

"See, and don't you dare put this on your nurfy teleshow, I am usually the Red Herring," said the girl as she led him down a long paneled corridor. "I was All State Red Herring back home two years in a row."

"Which state?"

"Well, Ohio. But even—"

"Ohio's a damn fine state. We have a lot of wonderful viewers there," he said. "Your coach isn't letting you go in as Herring, huh?"

"No, damn it. At the last minute he tells me I'm in tomorrow's starting lineup as Least Likely Suspect."

"Isn't that good? The Least Likely's usually the killer, so that means you—"

"Oh, nertz. We haven't used the standard Least Likely play in years." She gave him another disdainful scan. "But I suppose I oughtn't to tell you that, or you'll blab it to one of the opposition teams. We'll be going up against Portugal in the First Round of Murder Games."

"Stiff competition?"

"For little short curly-haired people, I guess, but ..." She halted at an oaken door with a makeshift *Pistol Range* sign tacked to it. "If you must talk to Wispy, she's in here."

As his forlorn escort wandered off, Jake

knocked on the door and went in, trailed by his vidcamera.

There was a plump, pretty blonde young woman standing just inside the entrance. She held a pistol in each hand. "You look older in person than you do on the wall," she said.

"It's this harsh northern light, Miss O'Ruddy."

Lowering both guns, Wispy looked him over. "Is that a rug?"

Smiling amiably, Jake patted his false hair. "Boy, you got a nice direct approach to life," he said with an approving chuckle. "I can hardly wait to capture it on—"

"Because if it's a hairpiece you ought to get a refund," continued the pudgy blonde, "and if it's your own hair, Mr. Shuster, I'd say you must be suffering from a severe deficiency disease."

"Well, I'll tell you. Television is a cutthroat business and the viewers, survey after survey indicates, prefer vidreporters with hair. Think about it. You never see a bald anchor—"

"I hope you aren't going to babble like this when you're doing the interview with me." She raised her right hand, aiming at the center of the room.

This was usually a dining room and target dummies had been placed in the dozen carved realwood chairs ringing the table.

Wispy fired a safeslug at one of the dummies,

hit it square in the chest and sent it collapsing off its chair.

"We ought to be taping this," Jake told his camera.

Nodding, the robot's lens swung around to take in the young woman. From inside a whirring began.

Jake requested, "Knock off another of those dummies, will you, Miss O'Ruddy."

She brought up her left hand. "Know anything about guns?"

"A bit. Why?"

"See any difference between this one and the one I just fired?" She turned, pointing the remaining gun at him.

"Wellsir, now you mention it, I sure do," he said. "The one you have aimed at my vitals isn't a safegun, it's a kilgun."

Wispy smiled. "Suppose you tell me who you really are and what you want," she suggested.

23

From the dining room window of the inn at the edge of town you could see the bleak gray chateau on the snowy hillside a mile away. That was where Wallace Wind, Hildy had just confirmed, was indeed residing at the moment. Even from here the black-clad ski guards who watched over the approaches to the tycoon's hideaway were visible, ten of them spotted around the place.

Hildy, toying absently with one of her blonde braids, sat alone at a carved oaken table. There was an untasted mug of cocoa resting in front of her.

Jake was more than fifteen minutes overdue.

"Ah, there you are, old gel. Ripping, ripping."

Steranko, in his Inspector Wayland-Stonebruce guise, was making his way through the crowded dining area.

"A bit thick," said Hildy as he sat down in one of the empty chairs at her table.

"Eh, wot? Not makin' fun of a chap's mode of speech, are you?"

"You're about twice as British as any Englishman."

"Don't knock a great bravura performance, kiddo." He picked up a menu. "Where's the master of the ménage?"

"Don't know."

Steranko asked, "Did you find out anything whilst nosing about?"

"Wind is definitely in his chateau yonder." She nodded at the window.

"That's the place, huh? All it needs is Ivanhoe to make it complete." He squinted out into the snowy afternoon. "Those lads in black whizzing about on the slopes are looking after things?"

"Each and every one armed with stunrifle, kilgun, and electroknife," she said. "There's also a force dome over the whole setup and a defense system against any airborne threats."

"Snug, but he doesn't sound too neighborly." The siphoner closed his menu. "I've learned that Dr. D will arrive in about an hour and a half."

"Doesn't give us much time." She glanced over at the arched entryway.

"Aw, you guys are used to hairbreadth schedules," he said. "Oh, and they had a medteam unstun dear Kevin. He, too, is now en route to this selfsame wonderland of whiteness. On a later flight."

"He's not as dangerous as Death, so . . ."

"Your order, sir?" inquired the frail old waiter who'd appeared beside her table.

"Jove, I believe I'll just have an order of fried *makkara*, a wedge of *omena* pie, mug of cocoa and . . . That'll jolly well do it, eh?" He looked toward Hildy. "Wish anything further, old thing?"

"Nope."

Bowing, the waiter departed.

Steranko fished a monocle from his pocket, inserted it in his left eye. "You know, I'm impressed by—"

"Wrong eye."

"Ah, yes, to be sure." He placed the lens in his right eye. "I was about to observe that it's impressive how you and Jake are always so concerned over each other's welfare. Such devotion touches the heart."

"You're very perceptive. I didn't . . . oh, here's Jake."

His wig a mite askew, his cheek sporting a new plazband, Jake was striding over to them.

"Hi, all," he greeted in his best Boxboy Shuster style. "Sorry to keep the gang waiting." He sat next to his wife.

Smiling, Hildy stroked his knee. "I was on the brink of worrying."

"Miss O'Ruddy proved to be a feisty and suspicious lass," Jake explained. "She got the silly notion I wasn't the true Boxboy, even tried to use a kilgun on me."

"You thwarted that."

"Actually, my camera robot did. He's got a stungun built in and is programmed to deck anybody who tries to do me wrong."

"Where's the wench at the moment, old bean?"

"Asleep out in my snowcar, under a thermoquilt," answered Jake. "I've got a controlbug planted on her."

"Then she can," asked Hildy, "get you inside the chateau?"

"Yep." He gave an affirmative nod. "Turns out she was due to drop in on WW this afternoon anyway. She is, just as Steranko surmised, carrying on with the old gent. I'm going along with her as her favorite media person and an old chum to boot."

"We've found out Dr. Death'll be arriving in less than two hours," said his wife.

Jake pushed back from the table. "Then we

better commence moving," he said, standing. "You two start rolling on your part of things."

"Be careful." Rising, Hildy kissed him quickly on the cheek.

Steranko stayed seated. "Surely there's time for all of us to partake of a hearty meal, perhaps even an after-dinner—"

"There isn't," said Jake.

"No wonder," said the siphoner, "you're both so skinny."

The android butler said, "Might one mention, Miss O'Ruddy, that you're looking a trifle peckish?"

"It's the tension before the games, Butterwick-23," said the mind-controlled blonde.

Turning his pink, plump face toward Jake, the butler said, "She's mistaken me for the butler in the Swedish chalet. He's Butterwick-23, whereas I am, and always have been, Butterwick-25."

"So?" Wispy shed her all-season greatcoat and tossed it to him. "It's hard to tell one poof from another."

"One is upset at having one's masculinity doubted, miss."

"Where's Wally?"

She and Jake were standing in the large, dark-paneled foyer of the Wind chateau. A broad staircase curved up to the next level.

"Might one first inquire as to who this gentleman is?"

"Oh, he's my old buddy Boxboy Shuster, from Int Wallvision. He's doing an in depth inter—"

"Mr. Wind loathes the news media in all its—"

"Boxboy isn't interested in Wally at all. He's doing me," she told the butler impatiently, "because of the Games."

"Even so, miss, one hesitates to admit a member of the fourth estate to—"

"Hey, listen, Butterwick-25." Jake put a friendly arm around the mechanical man's shoulders. "Ol' Boxboy doesn't want to make trouble for a soul. Nope, I can just as simply do my taping of the little lady down in town if . . ."

Klank!

Jake slapped a parasite controlbutton against the butler's metal and sinskin neck.

"One finds oneself at your service, sir."

"Okay, where's Wind?"

"As I was about to explain to Miss O'Ruddy," said Butterwick, "the master is unconscious."

"Why the hell is that?" inquired Wispy. "He knows damn well I was due to drop in this—"

"Ah, yes, but there has been a last-minute change of plans. In point of fact, one has been attempting to contact you by pixphone for the past hour and so inform you."

"He better have himself a damn good reason for—"

"It's the Brainz, Inc. people, miss."

Jake said, "Is Dr. Death here already?"

"No, sir, though we expect him shortly," replied the pink-faced butler. "He has, however, already sent two of his regional representatives here. They are, even as we speak, preparing the master for his mindspot session."

"They rendered him unconscious?"

"That they did. As one has had the process explained to one, sir, that is required."

"Shit," said Jake.

"Beg pardon, sir?"

"How the hell," said Jake, "am I going to warn him now?"

 **24**

Dr. Death asked, "Have you heard the one about the grizzly bear and the jack rabbit? Well, it seems. . . ."

The ambiance system at the Gnordling skyport dome was moderately on the fritz. A thin mist was drifting in ribbons over the tufftile floor and the snow hitting the plaz sections of the roof wasn't just melting but was collecting in pools and boiling and burbling like soup.

Unfazed, Dr. Vincent Death had paused after disembarking from his skyliner to chat with the ten or so media people who'd gotten wind of his arrival.

At the edge of the group circling him were Hildy and Steranko.

"I'll flit over to a pixphone," whispered the siphoner, "and alert Jake to the fact that Doc D has indeed come to town."

"Okay, but make sure you deliver the message only to him or to Wispy." Hildy twisted one of her braids around her forefinger. "Meanwhile I'll attend to stalling the good doctor."

Death was a modest-sized man, about five foot four. He had a pleasant, open face and wavy light hair. He wore a two-piece tan travsuit, carried a plazcase tucked under his arm. He had reached the punchline of his joke. ". . . so the grizzly bear wiped his rump with the rabbit."

The Int Wallvision robot laughed the loudest.

The thin young woman from Scansat made a politely rude noise. "Can you address yourself, sir, with a minimum of further buffoonery," she inquired, pushing nearer to him, "to the question of the deployment of itchmissiles in our Scandinavian Alliance Countries?"

Smiling, Dr. Death put his tokwatch to his ear. "I don't really have time for a detailed answer, honey," he replied. "Let me say, though, that while I am no longer associated with SafeWar Products as a consultant, I thoroughly approve of their so-called practical-joke approach to deterrence. Better an enemy army incapacitated by itching powder than by more deadly—"

"Pity," cut in a black reporter from AfroNews,

"you didn't feel that way, doctor, when you introduced Asthmaline into—"

"Asthmaline doesn't kill people, sonny. All it does is—"

"I can show you documents that prove more than two hundred and fifty—"

"That sort of reminds me of the story about Shapiro and his wife," said the doctor. "You folks know that one? Well, it seems . . ."

Hildy glanced toward the bank of pixphone alcoves across the dome. The mist was growing denser and she could just make out Steranko.

" '. . . Marcus, I have to. But you?' " concluded Dr. Death. The waves of his hair danced when he chuckled. "Well, folks, that's just about all the time I have for—"

"Oh, please, Dr. Death," called Hildy. "Do tell us the story about you and the Russian countess."

Death blinked, turned his attention to her. "Don't believe I know you, miss."

Hildy tilted her press badge toward him with her thumb. "Trutilda Quiller, sir, with the APA Newsservice."

"Yes, of course. Nice seeing you again, Tillie. Now, what was that you—"

"I've heard your anecdote about you and the Russian countess is a classic. Please, do, tell it."

"What we want to hear," said the angry

ScanSat woman, "is why well over five hundred itchmissiles are to be placed in our countries. There is absolutely—"

"As to the Asthmaline question, Dr. Death. Is it not true—"

"Wellsir," said Dr. Death, grinning at Hildy, "this all happened back when I was a young man in my native Pennsylvania. Like many a young lad before me I hadn't much money and when, one fine day, I met this beautiful Russian countess, and succeeded in persuading her to go to dinner . . ."

From the corner of her eye Hildy again checked the pixphones. Steranko didn't appear to be in any of the alcoves. High overhead the collected snow water was gurgling and bubbling.

" '. . . Oh, but I much prefer champagne,' the countess informed me when I suggested beer. Batting her beautiful, lustrous and limpid eyes at me, she went on to explain, 'When I drink champagne I am transported. After its first titillating bubbles reach my . . .' "

The mist was even thicker, swirling around Hildy. She scanned the dome, trying to spot Steranko.

"We've got him," explained a voice at her left. "And now . . . we've got you."

Hildy felt a sudden tingling in her rib cage and, before she could turn, she blacked out, tumbling to her knees on the misty floor.

" 'But beer,' she informed me, 'beer makes me fart.' " Dr. Death stared down at the fallen Hildy after he concluded the joke. "Let me through to her, folks, let me through. I'm a doctor."

Jake, accompanied by Butterwick the butler, moved quietly along the upper hallway.

Clearing his throat and stopping, the android pointed at an oaken door. "They're in there, sir."

"Knock, and do what I told you," whispered Jake.

"To hear is to obey, sir." He tapped on the wood.

This produced no response from within.

Butterwick tried again.

"What?" came an impatient voice.

"I fear, sir, we face a bit of an emergency."

"Such as?" The voice was nearer the door.

"The generators are about to go out, sir. Meaning there'll be not a bit of power for the entire—"

"How can one of the richest men in the world have a generator system that goes flooey?"

"Ah, sir, thereby hangs a tale," the butler said to the door. "Mr. Wind is, bless him, what is known in the upper echelons of international finance circles as a skinflint. He simply does not go first cabin when it comes to—"

"What about your auxiliaries?"

"About to blow as well, sir."

"Okay. I'll go take a look at the damn things. A Kirktronics tech ought to be able to ... Christ!" The lanky blond young technician had opened the door and noticed Jake.

"Hi." Jake sprang, hitting the fellow in the sternum with his elbow.

Zzzzzzummmmm!

Before the tech regained his balance, Jake used his stungun on him.

He then dived to the floral rug, rolled, rose by executing a skillful backflip and fired twice again.

Zzzzzzummmmmmm!

Zzzzzummmmmmm!

He dropped the other two Brainz, Inc. techs who were in the large bedchamber before they could even completely yank out their own weapons. Both had been going for kilguns.

Sprinting to the canopied bed, Jake took hold of the arm of the large, knobby old man stretched out on it. "Wind! Hey, wake up!"

"... immortality ... my mind shall live on ..." His eyes remained shut, his breathing shallow and wheezy.

"Awaken!"

Wallace Wind commenced snoring.

 **25**

Sitting back comfortably in the passenger seat of the skyvan, Dr. Death said, "This took place in London a few years ago and has to do with a gent named Bixby. One evening, during a pea-soup fog, I was strolling across one of the town's most impressive bridges when—"

"I've heard this yarn, doc," the husky vanpilot told him.

"You sure, Elroy?"

"Yeah."

"Bixby the bridge builder?"

"The punch line is, 'But suck one little—' "

"Damn, and that's one of my best gags, too. Where'd you hear it?"

"In grade school on Majorca II."

"It's a splendid joke."

"That it is, doc." The pilot spoke a series of passwords into his tokmike.

The van dropped safely down through the force dome over the Wind landing area next to the chateau.

"How about the one where the little shoplifter is stopped by the lady store detective?"

" 'Pockets, who's got pockets?' "

"That was a fine school you attended, my boy."

"It was."

"I don't suppose you have some favorite stories of your own you could pass along to me for—"

"Who's that coming out of the joint with a gnat up his toke?"

A door at the side of the chateau had come flapping open. Butterwick emerged on the run, arms waving.

Activating the door on his side of the cabin, Dr. Death stepped out into the chill afternoon. "What seems to be the trouble?"

"Do I have the pleasure of addressing Dr. Death?" The android hurried up to the side of the freshly landed van.

"I'm Vincent Death, yes. What exactly—"

"Lord love a duck! Who are those people sprawled out in the back of your van there?" Leaning around the doctor, the butler was staring into the skyvan. "Don't tell me they're having side effects, too?"

"A young lady and a young gentleman on my staff," said the doctor, shutting the door. "Napping after a busy morning. What other side effects are you alluding to?"

"Oh, haven't I made myself clear? It's the master, sir."

"Mr. Wind?"

"Indeed. I fear you may have a good deal to answer for," said the butler, moving toward the side entrance to the chateau. "Those lads you sent ahead of you have caused no end of—"

"I assure you my best men were assigned to this job. So that—"

"Be that as it may, that doesn't account for the spots."

"Spots?"

"If you'll be so good as to accompany me inside, doctor. You shall see what I mean."

Turning to the cab, Dr. Death called to the pilot. "Wait for me here, Elroy. Keep an eye on our . . . resting friends."

"Got you."

"Spots?" repeated Dr. Death, following Butterwick inside.

"Most of them are purple, sir. All over the master's poor old body."

"That's impossible. There are no side effects to the simple sleep drugs we use in our mindspot sessions." They moved along a long, shadowy hallway. "These spots, as you call them, are no doubt due to something else. A virus perhaps or—"

"Would a virus also account for the feathers?"

Dr. Death broke his stride. "Feathers?"

"Sprouted around his ankles and wrists shortly after your confederates began to—"

"These men are highly skilled technicians who—"

"Still, sir, one recognizes feathers when one sees them growing on the person of one's master." He slowed, halted before a door on the ground floor. "We've brought the master down here."

Dr. Death promised, "We'll soon get to the bottom of this." Opening the door for himself, he plunged into the room. "Now then, what's all this about . . . Ah!"

Wallace Wind was sitting in an ornate armchair, wide awake and facing the doctor. In a chair beside him sat a thickset bald man in a three-piece white bizsuit.

To Wind's right stood Jake, a stungun dangling in his hand. "I'm afraid," said Jake. "we've played a joke on you, doctor."

Wallace Wind tossed another realwood log on the blaze in the deep fireplace and prodded it.

He handed the poker over to Butterwick. "Bullshit, Vincent," he said.

Dr. Death was seated on the edge of a sofa. "Pace here is nothing but a cheap gumshoe," he said. "He is, I assure you, capable of faking the vidtapes and other data you claim he showed you. Why, he's in cahoots on this particular case with a man, a notorious character, known far and wide as Steranko the Siphoner. That nickname alone tells you exactly what sort of—"

"I just had a nice pixphone chat with Sylvie Kirkyard." The old tycoon returned to his chair. "Lucky Pace got me awake again. . . . He has quite a few slick tricks for accomplishing that. Yes, a pleasant conversation with Sylvie—"

"She's dead. The poor child passed away in GLA over—"

"Passed away with the help of Asthmaline, Vincent."

"Nonsense, Wind. My loyalty to the Kirkyard family is unquestioned and I would never . . . Ah, I see. You talked to that spurious android replica of the girl." Dr. Death chuckled, rubbing his palms together. "You and I know how easily an andy can be programmed to tell all sorts—"

"I've arrived where I am, Vincent, by paying attention to facts and figures," said Wind, "and also by playing hunches. The facts and figures Pace showed me seem damn convincing. And

so does the story that Sylvie Kirkyard tells."
He pressed a freckled hand against his broad
chest. "My hunch is the whole damn thing is
true."

"Hunches don't mean anything in—"

"Hunches, along with the stuff Pace has, may
just fix your wagon, Vincent," the old man told
him. "Which is why I invited Mr. Amberson to
drop in."

Death frowned at the bald man. "I don't believe I know the—"

"I'm with the International Police Commission, Dr. Death," explained Amberson. "I work
out of the Finland station and, if you don't
mind, I'd like you to accompany me there now."

"Impossible. I have urgent—"

"I have the papers needed to detain you."
Amberson produced sheets of yellow and blue
faxpaper, several white and green plaz cards
from his coat pocket. "We can go at once."

"Wind, I am . . . astounded . . . yes, astounded
that you'd believe a man like Pace here rather
than—"

"Better go along quietly," suggested Jake.

"Before you get too smug, Pace, you ought to
know that I picked up your wife and Steranko
at the skyport." Smiling, Dr. Death stood up.
"Should anything happen to me—"

"Where are they?" Jake moved toward him.

"Ahum," said Butterwick. "One has a notion,

Mr. Pace. The doctor has two unconscious people, who might just be your lady and this other gentleman, in the back of his skyvan. Perhaps you'd best have a look."

"Yep, I will." Jake headed for the doorway.

Sighing, Dr. Death turned to Amberson. "Well," he said, "this reminds me of the story about. . . ."

 **26**

After rubbing his fingers together a few times Jake began playing the piano in the family room. He hummed as he played.

He went through "Jelly Roll Blues" and was in the midst of "Some Sweet Day" when he heard a thumping on the ramp leading down.

Leaving the piano bench quickly, Jake grabbed the stungun he kept attached to the side of the piano.

"Oh, I'm not the demographer . . . and I ain't the demographer's son," sang John J. Pilgrim as he made his way into the room. "But I—"

"What brings you here?" asked Jake, reluctantly hanging up the weapon.

"Not any deep and abiding affection for

you, squire," responded the tipsy attorney. He crouched, looked around the room. "Where's the lame chimpanzee?"

"Hum?"

"The one I just heard dancing on your key-board."

"State your business," advised Jake.

Pilgrim started frisking himself, probing into the lumpy pockets of his rumpled suit. "My client, who may well be suffering from a case of severe dippiness ... Ah, here's that flask of Chateau Discount Sparkling Sherry with Malted Milk added for zest. Thought I lost that when I got rolled last week in an alley out in Albany, Califor—"

"Which client?"

"Sylvie Kirkyard." He located two further plazflasks before coming across the envelope that was his goal. "Here, a bonus."

Jake extracted the envelope from between the lawyer's fingertips. "Have you changed this suit since you were wallowing in that alley?"

"I'm not the Beau Brummell you are."

Jake scanned the contents of the fat envelope. "One hundred thousand dollars."

"Lot more than your whole carcass is worth."

"When folks pay Odd Jobs, Inc. they are also paying Hildy, remember."

"True. She's worth it." Pilgrim took out his

rediscovered flask of Sparkling Sherry. "I'd like a receipt for the dough."

"Hildy handles that. She's upstairs baking—"

"Cookies. I know. She even tried to foist one on me," said the lawyer while uncapping his wine. "You two are the cookie bakingest bunch it's ever been my—"

"How's Sylvie faring?"

"She's doing marvelously well," Pilgrim answered. "I got her declared her own legal heir. She and her brother are now running the whole Kirktronics shebang, cleaning house right and left. That's the honest brother, Ross Kirkyard."

"Never met him."

"You haven't missed an edifying experience. He's not even as interesting as Kevin, the crooked one."

"Kevin still in custody?"

When Pilgrim nodded, his wine spurted some from the mouth of his flask. "Kevin, Dr. Sanhamel and Dr. Death himself are all languishing in the International Police Commission bastille in Stockholm."

"Think they'll go to prison?"

"Maybe. But they're going to spend a lot of dough trying to keep out," said the lawyer. "The important thing is, they won't try to hurt Sylvie again or take over Kirktronics. That's something."

Jake set the money atop the piano. "Tell Sylvie we appreciate the bonus."

"The lass admires you. If I was on the other side I'd use that as evidence for getting her declared legally goofy." He took one more swig before capping his wine and hiding it away. "I'll be departing. Mayhap I'll see you and the missus at the wedding."

"What wedding?"

"Sylvie's. She's marrying that nitwit cartoonist Higby next month."

"Can androids do that?"

"Androids who have me for a lawyer sure as hell can."

"He really loved her," said Jake, shaking his head.

"Most of these mixed marriages don't work," said Pilgrim, heading for the ramp out. "But, what the heck, it's the closest thing to a happy ending we can get under the circumstances." He took his leave.

Returning to the piano, Jake noodled a nameless blues for a few minutes.

Then he headed upstairs, calling out, "Is that booze-soaked shyster gone, Hildy?"

From the kitchen she answered, "Long since."

He found her in there, flour dusting her cheek. "I have a suggestion," he said from the doorway.

"We're always open to suggestions."

"Let's take the afternoon off and go to bed."

Hildy considered. "Are we celebrating the bonus?"

"That and the fact I'm not married to an android."

Hildy smiled at him. "Either reason is sufficient," she said.

DAW

The adventures of Dray Prescot on the planet Kregen of the double-star Antares is the greatest interplanetary series of its kind since Edgar Rice Burroughs and Edward E. Smith stopped writing. Now the greatest of these novels, a powerful trilogy, has been specially reprinted by popular demand.

THE KROZAIR CYCLE

Covers by Michael Whelan! Interior Illustrations!

1. **THE TIDES OF KREGEN**   (UE2034—$2.75)
   Illustrated by Michael Whelan.

2. **RENEGADE OF KREGEN**   (UE2035—$2.75)
   Illustrated by Jack Gaughan.

3. **KROZAIR OF KREGEN**   (UE2036—$2.75)
   Illustrated by Josh Kirby.

As told by Dray Prescot himself to Alan Burt Akers.
Heroic fantasy at its very best!

DAW

Presenting C. J. CHERRYH

Two Hugos so far—and more sure to come!

The Morgaine Novels
- [ ] GATE OF IVREL   (#UE1956—$2.50)
- [ ] WELL OF SHIUAN   (#UE1986—$2.95)
- [ ] FIRES OF AZEROTH   (#UE1925—$2.50)

The Faded Sun Novels
- [ ] THE FADED SUN: KESRITH   (#UE1960—$3.50)
- [ ] THE FADED SUN: SHON'JIR   (#UE1889—$2.95)
- [ ] THE FADED SUN: KUTATH   (#UE1856—$2.75)

- [ ] FORTY THOUSAND IN GEHENNA (#UE1952—$3.50)
- [ ] DOWNBELOW STATION   (#UE1828—$2.75)
- [ ] MERCHANTER'S LUCK   (#UE1745—$2.95)
- [ ] PORT ETERNITY   (#UE1769—$2.50)
- [ ] WAVE WITHOUT A SHORE   (#UE1957—$2.95)
- [ ] SUNFALL   (#UE1881—$2.50)
- [ ] BROTHERS OF EARTH   (#UE1869—$2.95)
- [ ] THE PRIDE OF CHANUR   (#UE1694—$2.95)
- [ ] SERPENT'S REACH   (#UE1682—$2.50)
- [ ] HUNTER OF WORLDS   (#UE1872—$2.95)
- [ ] HESTIA   (#UE1680—$2.25)
- [ ] VOYAGER IN NIGHT   (#UE1920—$2.95)
- [ ] THE DREAMSTONE   (#UE2013—$2.95)
- [ ] THE TREE OF SWORDS AND JEWELS (#UE1850—$2.95)
